Twisted Images

HER LAST BREATH WHILE LOOKING IN THE MIRROR

Erica Lynn Collins

Order this book online at www.trafford.com
or email orders@trafford.com

Most Trafford titles are also available at major online book retailers.

Print information available on the last page.

ISBN: 978-1-4907-5830-5 (sc)
ISBN: 978-1-4907-5832-9 (hc)
ISBN: 978-1-4907-5831-2 (e)

Library of Congress Control Number: 2015905500

Trafford rev. 02/24/2017

 www.trafford.com

North America & international
toll-free: 844-688-6899 (USA & Canada)
fax: 812 355 4082

I was once a good girl. After a while, I said, "Why should I be fair to these men who are not fair to themselves or to women?" I was in a relationship, where every time he saw a face, he would want to try that woman. I forgave him and forgave him until I got tired of believing things would change. One mess up was enough, but two, three, four, and five? He kept going on and on. It was too much. I thought to myself, *Why put up with this?* I cried my pillows wet at night. I hurt for days, weeks, and months. I even received text messages, phone calls, looks and even fake smiling faces, and he said his hellos and byes by hoes he was sleeping with, and some did not even care he had a woman.

He spoiled me with the finest things in life Michael Kors purses, Louboutin, Coach, watches, clothing, stilettos, he got my hair and nails done, cars, and even my favorite Coco Chanel perfumes. Even the finest things couldn't keep me happy when I knew he was out doing me wrong. I like my man to myself, and don't like to share him with anyone else. I went to church faithfully. I cooked, cleaned, and did everything for him, without him having to ask. I did everything sexually for him—from making love, to fucking hard, soft, long, sucking dick, getting that dick up, riding his ass, going one, two, three, four, five rounds, making sure I'd be the one who gets it up and puts it back on flat. If he wanted a stripper, I was that stripper. If he wanted a prostitute, I was that prostitute. If he wanted a schoolgirl, a cheerleader or a porn star, I was that. I was that freak in the sheets and that lady in the streets. I was his woman with nice hips, curves, and the whole nine yards. Yes, I was Sasha. I was whatever Tristan wanted or needed. I did it.

After some years, he started feeling himself, knowing he had a beautiful woman at home, a woman that men pray for, but I think I was too good of a woman for Tristan. He started sleeping with anything and everything that walks. Some of the women that he slept with made me check myself twice a week and not every three to six months. He just made me sick to my stomach, and of course, Tristan had a story to tell—he didn't mean to sleep with her or he thought the ugly hoe wouldn't open her mouth. Yeah right. My name is Sasha, not dumb bitch, because even a trash can hoe can't hold ice water. She'll drink it up and swallow the ice whole before it can even melt. That's how thirsty those hoes are, but enough with those hoes. Let's get started on Sasha and how her life changed.

After exploring life watching others, from married men, men with girlfriends, to single men, just watching the actions of people and how their lives are filled with lies, betrayal, not trust or whatsoever, and the enemy that stands beside them, who is the best friend that's fucking the husband, wife, girlfriend, or boyfriend, I, Sasha, got tired of being lonely. I started going to clubs, bars, and even on small dates, thinking it would ease my loneliness and keep my mind from thinking crazy things (laughing out loud), but it did not. I went home by myself, I was so lonely, and took a bath by myself too. I stared at my naked body, lit candles by the tub, and touched myself. I sucked my fingers, and pinched my nipples, rubbing ice cubes around my nipples. I took my hand and chased the dripping, cold water from the ice down to my body and into my belly button. I caressed myself with the other hand in my pussy, and made myself soaking wet. Ooooh boy, that felt good.

Days and months went by, and my girls called me up to go to this really big all-white party. I didn't feel like going anywhere at first, but then I thought to myself, *Hell, why not?* So I went shopping, got my hair done into some tight worn curls, had my nails, feet, eyebrow, and eyelashes done, and went home to get my beauty rest for about an hour. The clock struck eight o'clock in the evening. I started taking my shower, and while in the shower,

I started thinking of caressing myself again, but I said to myself, "Not tonight, Sasha." Because if I do, I will fuck myself so hard, I'll put myself to sleep. That's how good I was, espccially when it comes to having a really good orgasm, but I was just tired of being lonely.

I rubbed my body down with body butter and slipped on my see-through knee-length all-white body-con silk dress with my all-white thong underneath. I then put on my clear crystal dangle earrings with the matching necklace and applied my gray contact lenses. I placed light makeup on my face and applied my ruby-red lipstick onto my big soft full lips. My phone rang. It was my girlfriends asking where was I. While I slipped on my five-inch Louboutin stilettos and walked toward the door, I told them I was on my way out. I grabbed my wrist purse and my car keys and headed out to the party.

As I arrived at the party, there were so many cars and so many people and front door services. I didn't even have to park. I called my girls and told them I was out front. When I stepped into the scene, everybody was watching. My heart was beating and beating. Fine men were here, there, and everywhere. I felt like I was in men heaven. When I was in a relationship with my man, other men didn't even exist. They were a blur in my eyesight, but now, I get to look around. *Yes, yes, yes. Men are here, there, oh my goodness! They're everywhere!*

So my girls and I started moving around the club. I was introduced to numerous people—from my friends' friends to their friends and to just random people. I was sipping on a glass of red wine when a guy approached me and tried to introduce himself. My mind was on the man across the floor, staring me down, with the muscles and the tight-fitting shirt. He had a chocolate fitted, tight body, drinking his beer and staring directly into my face. As he kept staring, he began walking over to me and asked, "May I have this dance?" I didn't even know the other guy was still talking. My mind had wonder off on Mr. Sexyman. As the music played, we danced to the beat. His name was Victor, worked at a refinery and he had no kids and have never been married.

We conversed that whole night. The time went by, and it was close to the party ending. I am a woman that does not like to stay until the lights come on, because it will be too crowded while trying to leave, and things happen in the parking lot after the club and I would not try to know the outcome. I hugged my girls and told them I was leaving, and Victor walked me to the front, but as we stood there waiting for my car, my hormones started kicking. My panties started getting wet, my nipples started poking out, and my pussy started throbbing. I knew it wasn't the liquor. I just needed my flames to be put out by the real thing. My mind was racing for some loving. Out of the blue, I asked Victor if he wanted to come over and keep me company. Victor said, "Of course."

As he got into his vehicle, I got into mine, and this stranger followed me home, into my house, and into my bed, where no time was wasted. We made love, we had sex, and we went round after round until all my energy was gone. The time I saw on the clock when we lay down was 1:25 a.m., and now, as we finished up, it's 6:49 a.m. As I lay there, I thought to myself, *What have I done?* Then I said to myself, *Well, I am single, and he is too, and I can tell by the way we had sex that I wasn't the only one that needed it.* As his sexy ass lay asleep, snoring, I slept on the side of him with one eye open and the other one closed. Like I said, my hormones were jumping, but I still didn't know this dude. *Sleep, Daddy, because you have one more hour and your ass got to go.*

I was awakened by the sunrise that shined through the blinds and into my face, and when I looked over to my left, Victor was gone—no letter, no good-byes, no signs that he was even here. Nothing was left behind but the smell of sex. I opened the blinds and raised the windows just to get a fresh breeze from outside while I started to freshen myself up and then do some house cleaning. My phone rang. *Oh no, he is not calling me.* It was Tristan, my ex. I did not answer. We did not have anything to talk about. My phone rang again, and it's Tristan again. I picked it up, asking, "What, Tristan?"

Tristan said, "Sasha, I miss you. I need you back in my life."

I said, "Hold up. Don't fix your mouth to tell me shit like that because when I needed you to be there, you wasn't. You choose to be in the streets. What is the matter? You done swept through all the hoes? Or did you catch the flu through some bad pussy?"

Tristan said, "Baby, no I need to come home. I don't have anywhere to go."

"Come home, Tristan? When a roof was given to you, you burned that mutherfucka down with your lies, cheating, betrayal, and your pitiful ass self. You can't come back here. Better yet, lose my number. You're no longer welcome to even say hi or bye."

Click.

I began preparing my meal for the day—smothered roast, gravy, rice, pinto beans with sausage, and baked butter corn bread. Then I heard my doorbell ring. It was my girls with some other chicks and three guys. They had coolers filled with beer and wine and had their swimwear on, yelling, "Party over here! Party over here!"

I asked my friend Ariel who were the men and the extra chicks, because I have never seen them before and this is my house. I needed to know who these bitches were. So Ariel introduced them. Two of the ladies were her cousins, and the other one was a friend of her cousins, and the guys were their boyfriends.

"Okay, so let's get this fucking party started!" I yelled as I turned on the music jamming "Pour It Up" by RiRi as I started popping bottles.

I went into my bedroom to change into a swimsuit, not thinking to shut my room door, and one of the guys had gotten lost looking for the bathroom. As I was halfway naked, I saw him from the side mirror watching me. My heart started beating, my hormones started jumping, and my pussy started throbbing. I started sliding my panties down slowly. I started winding my hips in circles, moving to the rhythm of the music that was playing, touching and feeling myself. As I danced with my eyes closed, I felt two hands grip my boobs and a hard dick pressing up against me. I turned around and started kissing him from his head to his waist, pulling his swim trunks down, and he picked me up and placed me on the dresser as his face went below my waist, licking and sucking on my pearl tongue.

"Ouch! Give it to me!" I said as he placed his nine-inch dick into me while sucking on my nipples. My flames had risen so high I pushed him down on the floor and rode that dick as he stroked back harder and harder while gripping my waist so tight. Oh my goodness, that fuck felt so fucking good! After we were done, I told him to get out before someone catches him up here, and he left to return downstairs. Hell, I didn't even get his name, and hell, I didn't need it.

I took a shower and put on my swimsuit and returned to the party. We partied, danced, ate, and drank, and as I was sipping on my drink, the guy whom I had just got through fucking stared at me for a hot minute without even blinking. So to distract this fucker, I told them I was going to go pop some popcorn so that we can have popcorn and movie outside.

As I entered the house, the other guy was at my kitchen table, eating a plate of food. I had opened the cabinet to get popcorn and could not reach it, so he helped me get it down. As he pressed against me, oh my goodness, he was packing too. I started the popcorn in the popcorn maker, and the dude said to me, "I never got your name."

I said, "Sasha, and yours?"

He said, "Justin."

As the first batch was ready, I started pouring the butter on the popcorn. As I poured, Justin picked up some popcorn and started putting it in my mouth. As he did, I started sucking his fingers, and he picked me up and placed me on the counter as we made soft and sweet sex. I was on fire. When we were done, I had him bring the popcorn outside while I ran upstairs to take a shower.

While taking a shower, I heard my door open. It was one of the chicks that had come with my friend Ariel. I asked if I can help her, and she said yes, taking off her clothes and slowly walking to the shower, saying, "I saw you with my cousin's boyfriend."

I said, "Okay. He was helping me with the popcorn."

She got into the shower, placing her hands around my waist, saying, "No. You two was fucking."

As she started kissing me, I started kissing her, and we made love to each other, and little did she know that I fucked her boyfriend too. I just didn't get his name. Oh boy, what a party.

Well, that night ended, and I slept late. The next day, I was running late for work. When I arrived at work, I saw flowers on my desk and a basket of fruits. I had no idea who sent them, but let's see. "To Ms. Sasha. From your secret lover."

I hate it when I have to guess who the fuck sent me gifts. I asked my secretary who sent the gifts. She said, "A dark-skinned muscular guy dropped them off." All I could think of was Victor. What can I say, he is charming.

After locking my office up for the night, I started walking to my car, and a black limousine pulled up and the window was lowered. It was Victor.

"Hi, Victor. What are you doing here?"

Victor replied, "Coming to take a lovely lady out for dinner prepared by Victor himself."

I replied "Oh really?" as Victor stepped out the limousine to open the door for me to enter.

"How was your day at work, Ms. Sasha?" Victor asked.

"It was busy," I replied, "and thanks for the gifts."

"You're welcome," Victor replied.

Champagne was served in the limousine as we rode to our destination, which was a really nice big house. Let's just see how the inside is set up. I always remember this: Don't judge a book by its cover. What looks good might not be good, and what looks bad may not be bad.

As we exited the limousine, we entered into this nice big house.

"Oh my goodness, this is nice, Victor."

There were rose petals everywhere, candles, dim lights, maids, and nice, slow music playing. *I think I am falling in love.* As we sat at the dinner table, we drank homemade wine. The food was delicious, and we talked about everything. Victor then walked me into a room with nice fluffy pillows on the floor, a lit fireplace, strawberries, two champagne glasses, and the sound of a falling spring water flowing. *This man is romantic.*

Victor massaged me from my head to my toes, and he ate strawberries and whip cream off my body. As we lay, we forgot about everything and everybody else, including time. We made love, and he licked me in all the right places, and in return, I sucked his dick so fucking good his toes curled, and I let Victor have my body any way he wanted it.

The next day, I was awakened by the smell of breakfast—bacon, eggs, grits, butter biscuits, and a cup of green tea. *Yes, this man is a keeper.* After we were done eating breakfast, I needed to go home to freshen myself up and to change some more clothes, but instead, Victor asked me not to leave. We made love again, and then he took me shopping.

Victor said, "Get anything you want."

He bought me so many outfits, with new stilettos to match it, and he even bought me two designer handbags. The total cost of everything was over $3,000.

As Victor and I were walking in the mall, a little girl ran up to Victor yelling "Daddy! Daddy!" My mind froze for a hot minute, then I said to the little girl, "Darling, you have the wrong daddy."

The little girl looked at me and said, rolling and popping her neck, "No, lady. This is my daddy."

I looked at Victor. He was quiet, and not a single word came out of his mouth. The little girl grabbed Victor's hand, pulling him, and that's when Victor responded, "Hi, sweetie. What are you doing here?"

The little girl said, "Me, Damion, Susie, Drameka, and Mom came in today."

I said, "Victor, what is going on?"

Then the little girl said, "Daddy, who is this lady?"

Before Victor could answer, a lady walked up and said, "Hey, honey," and hugged and kissed him.

After seeing all that, I politely grabbed all my shopping bags and didn't ask any question. Victor had four kids and a wife, who had been out of town on a vacation. All I can say is that I did enjoy the time that was spent and also the shopping spree, but still, in all, this muthafucka lied. It's all good though. Life must go on. I caught a cab home, and later on that night, I took a long jog to not think about Victor because his sex was so good. If I would see him, my body would be magnetic and would stick right to him.

The next morning, I was awakened by a phone call from Victor, which I ignored. I took a warm bath and soaked to get the scent of Victor off me. While in the tub, my doorbell rang. *Damn,* I said to myself, *people don't call no more before they come over.* As I grabbed my dry-off towel, the doorbell rang and rang. I then put on my robe and peeped through the peephole. It was my best friend Ariel. I opened the door, and Ariel rushed in.

"Sasha, get your ass dressed, girl. We are going to the biggest barbecue, horseback riding, just one big party," she said as she handed me an invitation.

I slipped on my stonewashed high-waist cut-up shorts with holes in them and my pink-and-brown rhinestone belt with my tight muscle T-shirt, and I slid on my brown cowgirl boots and my brown cowgirl hat, and I was going to go eat me some barbecue, ride a horse, and who knows, I might meet a cowboy.

As Ariel and I were leaving from my house, an unfamiliar white Lexus was parked outside across from my home. As Ariel and I started to load up in my car, a voice of a woman called, "Sasha."

I looked back, and it was the woman in the white Lexus, and she said, "Yes, hoe. I know everything about you, how you fucked my man, how you had the nerve to come into my home and in my bed. Yes, bitch. I know all about you. I can't and I won't beat your ass right now because I have to meet my husband, Victor, and my kids for lunch, but I promise you I will whoop your ass, and you can count on that." She drove off.

I was puzzled because I knew he had to tell her something about me and she had known where I live. Victor probably did not mention how he told me he didn't have a wife or any kids. Now I was in the mind of his wife.

As Ariel and I arrived at the barbecue, we got out, and they took our invitations at the gate and handed each one of us a horse to ride. We had to ride horses through the trail to get to the other side where the party, the food, and the party people were, which was a big house and a big barnyard in the back. Loco Zydeco was playing, and there were different desserts, foods, drinks, and nice-looking men, white men and black men. It was a well-organized party.

Ariel and I started drinking and dancing, and other women started dancing along with us. We danced all night and drank all night, and we met lots of people. I went to sit down to have a drink, and a white guy approached me. He was sexy, and he was thirty-two years of age. His name was Paul. We talked and laughed, and then he asked if I was enjoying myself, and I said, "Yes, it's very nice here."

He replied, "I put a lot of money into this place, and every year, I try to give the biggest party ever, when I have the free time."

I said, "Well, you did a great job."

Paul said, "Thanks," and then he asked if I wanted to take a walk and see the rest of the property.

I said, "Of course."

As we walked through every inch of the house and outside and through the stables where he kept his horses, he started placing his hands on my booty, and I saw that the white man had liked him some caramel Sasha.

We both then jumped on horses and raced around the track, and of course, I was the first one back (laughing out loud). I don't know why men think they have to let the woman win. Paul helped me off my horse, and he ended up slipping, trying to hold all this booty. Poor thing. With all those muscles, he couldn't pick up a 125-pound petite woman. Paul and I both laughed, and he said, "I did that on purpose, because it's something about you that I like."

As he started kissing my neck and tongue-kissing, Paul went to rubbing on my legs and caressing my body. Next thing I knew, Paul was fucking me doggy style in a barnyard, pulling my hair so damn hard and fucking me so damn hard I screamed Victor's name out loud. Paul asked who the hell Victor was as he stroked even harder, pulling my hair.

I said to him as I turned around, "It's a name I want to call you because you look like you can be a victor, better yet, you fuck like a black man." As I climbed on top of him, riding his huge pink cock sideways, upside down, and backward and stroking his dick so hard, Paul's eyes were rolling in the back of his head. I had to ask if he was all right.

He said in his country voice, "Hell yeah, darling. I haven't felt sex like this in forever," as he gripped both of his hands on my ass cheek. He gripped so hard I felt his pulse beating fast.

When Paul and I had finished having sex, we both took a shower in the barnyard and freshened back up and then returned to the party. I started partying back and had a few more drinks with my friends. Everyone then started line dancing, and that's when some guy got behind me, whispering in my ear, "Why don't you have dinner with me tomorrow night, and I'll pick you up around eight o'clock sharp?" He slid his card in my side pockets as he walked away. I just seem to attract so many men. What have I been missing?

I ended up getting a funny feeling that someone was watching me, and as I looked up, I noticed Paul was standing in the corner of the dance floor, looking straight at me with a weird stare. Paul started pointing at me, pulling his index finger in a back-and-forward motion, meaning, "come here." As I walked over to Paul, he started digging in my pocket and took the card out that the guy from the dance floor had slid in my pocket, and he said, "We're not going to start that. You belong to me now. No one else can have what's mine."

I then said to Paul in his ear, "Let's get some things straight, white boy. Sasha don't belong to no one, and grown folks don't catch feelings in one night. Now you got some free pussy tonight. Now you take that, and you run with it, but nothing is owned by you all because you got to touch it, feel it, or lick it. I came here by myself, and I leave here by myself. So get your fucking head on straight, and shut the fuck up, and learn to take pussy when it's given to you."

Paul then whispered to me if he could speak to me in private. As we exited the party area, I followed Paul up some stairs where there were nice paintings hung on it. They looked like thousand-dollar paintings. I didn't remember this side of the house. Anyway, this guy was loaded. Paul and I entered a bedroom where he started shouting at me about things he didn't like and how this and that was going to be, and before you knew it, he had pinned me against the wall, gripping my neck so hard, and said in a deep, angry tone, "If you ever fix your lips to talk back, I will remove them from your pretty little face."

I wanted to scream, but Paul had my neck squeezed so tight I could barely breathe, so I started slapping and hitting him, trying to make him stop, but Paul took my punches as if he didn't even feel them. My heart started beating fast, and my mind just went blank. Paul had squeezed my neck so tight that I passed out completely.

I then awakened the next morning. I wasn't in my own bed or in my own nightclothes. I was in this fancy big-sized bed bigger than a king bed, and I had on some expensive silk lace top and bottom lingerie. I stepped out of the bed, whomsoever's bed, and looked out the window. I was still at the home where the party was given, and I thought about the crazy white boy Paul.

I have to get out of here. I looked around for my clothes. I did not see them or my shoes, my purse, or my phone. I then went to open the door and peeped around a corner. It was quiet as a mouse. I started tiptoeing through the huge, quiet house, shakily going down the stairs and into the kitchen, and I still didn't see anyone. I then spotted my car keys hanging from the key hook by the door, and I took off running full speed out the side door, but I ran into a parking lot full of nice cars, except mine wasn't there. I had forgotten we had ridden a horse all the way up here from the faraway front entrance. *Why do rich, crazy folks always have to be the ones with the houses way in the back? Damn, why do shit have to be so complicated?*

I ran to the barnyard in lingerie and barefoot. I was scared and nervous. I couldn't stop shaking. I had used an ax and popped the lock to one of the horse gates, and I hopped on and took off toward the front entrance. I saw my car, but as I got closer to the entrance, I could tell that it was a code-locked gate. My heart dropped, and I knew I was in some trouble. My nerves had gotten bad, and I started to cry, and that's when I heard over a speaker, "Sasha, babe, come back home, honey. We can talk this over."

I instantly started thinking. I never jumped a fence, but this one, I will climb. I started climbing, and all I could hear was Paul's voice yelling through the speakers, "Sasha! Sasha! Get your ass back here now!" I was already over the fence. I started up my car and burned rubber, going to a speed of 130, scared for my life. I won't be going to another party for a while.

I returned home, shaking, and locked every door there was, and I ran a hot bath and soak. I soaked for hours and cried at the same time. After I bathed, I lay in my bed and slept the whole day through.

Another day had come, and I got up and slipped on some clothes and went to cancel my phone and purchased a new phone. I then called my friend Ariel and asked her if she could meet me at a restaurant for a cup of coffee and breakfast and that I needed to talk to her and tell her what had happened. Ariel and I met up, and I told her everything. Ariel stayed over at my house for a couple of days, and I was well rested at last.

Daylight had come, and Ariel and I went out for some breakfast and went grocery shopping, and I ran into Victor's wife again, who had pushed my grocery cart with her bucket and said "Hoe!" out loud and kept on strolling. Ariel had told me not to worry about it, but I had every bit to worry about knowing that I was the innocent one that was caught up in this mess. I didn't have a clue about her, and I don't understand why women always point fingers at the other women without hearing the other side. This bitch wasn't trying to ask or hear anything. Anyways, I tried to keep myself calm. I didn't like the drama.

Later that day, I dropped Ariel off to her car and went on to continue shopping for my house. When I returned home, I went into my house, and Victor was in my living room. He had given me a scare. I asked Victor why the hell he was in my house and how he got in. Victor never answered my questions. The only thing he asked was if he could explain himself.

I said, "Hell no, and I think you should leave."

Victor got up and said, "You think I should leave?"

I put my bags down and asked, "How clear do you need me to be? Get the fuck out my house, Victor."

Victor just started walking toward me. *Oh gosh.* As he got closer, I couldn't resist looking at his fine chocolate self. Victor had gotten so close he started kissing me, and chemistry set in fast. It mixed so well. The love we were making sounded so sweet. What can I say? Good dick makes a woman accept and do just about anything.

Later on that night, I needed a strong drink, but I had to work with what I had, and I ended up drinking two whole bottles of wine and passed out on the sofa in my living room. I was put to bed real quick.

The next morning, I went to work, and my secretary told me that the new doctor had started today and that he was sitting in my office. I entered my office, and I introduced myself as Dr. Sasha, the head doctor in charge at the facility, and he sat there, telling me about his experience, and handed me a folder of all information about himself.

His name was Dr. Castile. Dr. Castile visited me in my office two times that day and asked me several business questions in the same day, and we worked side by side with most of our patients. Later on that night, while closing, Dr. Castile asked if he could walk me out to my car, and I gave him a look like "Hell no."

He laughed and said, "No, I want to walk you to your car because that's what a man's supposed to do, and that no woman should ever walk alone."

I thought that was sweet, so of course, I let him. He even opened my car door for me. *Aww, how sweet.*

Dr. Castile then said, "Hopefully we can have a cup of coffee one day."

I replied, "I have a coffeemaker in my office," looking at his shiny bald-headed sexy ass.

Dr. Castile laughed and said, "No, Dr. Sasha. I am talking about you being my coffee in my cup."

My mouth dropped as he walked away, saying, "You have until tomorrow to think about it." And his number was in my briefcase pocket. *Oh shit, I am in trouble,* I thought to myself, because I had known that he was going to get these cookies.

Yep, that morning in my office, we had sex on my desk. It was great, and from that day on, Dr. Castile and I continued fucking— in my office, on hospital beds, in restrooms, in supply closets, in the parking garage, and even under the desk in the conference room. I went to work faithfully every day, and each day, Castile and I spent time together eating out, having picnics, walking on the beach, going on vacations and to parties, and at bedtime. We had become a couple. I felt like that happiest woman alive. I found love again.

A few weeks later, I had taken a shower and went to bed. I went to sleep alone that night because Castile had to work a double. Usually, he would be right here by my side. I was awakened by the sound of a flicking lighter, and it was Paul sitting on my chair at the foot of my bed with the stare of a madman. I was so scared and told him if he did not leave, I would scream or call the police.

Paul yelled, "Bitch! You left me! You betrayed me, Sash! You had me looking all around for you up until I noticed that your purse was there, along with your identification in it! You fucked me, and I gave you my time and day, and you just left me"

I moved slowly out the bed, saying, "Paul, it was just one day."

Paul started yelling, "Bitch, one day is all it takes!"

I said to Paul, "I am sorry. I didn't think it was going to be taking this far."

Paul yelled, "Shut the hell up!" as he started walking toward me with a machete on the side of him.

My heart started beating fast. Tears rolled down my eyes, and my whole body was shaking. I was so, so scared.

Paul said, "Oh no, don't cry, Sash, Ms. I-Fucking-Use-People-and-Just-Walk-Away."

I said to Paul, "It wasn't like that at all. I was scared."

Paul then said, "Scared of what, Sasha? We had a little disagreement, and you got scared?"

I said, "Paul, you choked me until I passed out."

Paul then said, "All you had to do was not talk back to me and obey me, and you didn't. Just like I ask you not to leave out my gate, and you left anyway. Little you just leapt my fence."

I started running toward my door. I didn't get far because Paul had pulled me from the back, pulling me by my hair across the floor and into my bed. As I cried out loud for help, he slapped me in my face and told me to shut up as he placed that sharp machete knife to my neck, saying, if only I had listened to him, we would not be in this position. He started scrolling the knife down my body, cutting my nightclothes off my body. He pressed the knife against my private area, saying, "If I can't have you, nobody can."

I then started saying, "Paul, I was just scared. I was confused and scared of being hurt." I was trying to get his mind off killing me because I felt that I was going to die. I then told Paul as tears rolled down my face, "Whatever you want, I will do it. Whatever you want, but please don't kill me."

Paul started backing off me as he sat back into a chair and said, "Come here, Sasha my love."

I started walking toward him slowly, watching the door at the same time, thinking to run again, but my body was shaking. I feared for my life, too scared to make the run. Paul started taking off his shirt and unzipping his pants, pulling out his dick, telling me to suck on it. As I kneeled down to start giving Paul head, he gripped my hair and said, "Bitch, if you bite me or try anything stupid, I will kill you and cut out your heart for keepsake."

I then had no other thoughts but to do as I was told. From there, we had sex, and that night, we went six rounds. I was tired, exhausted, drained. Paul said if I told anybody about what had happened, he would find me faster than my eye could blink. Then he kissed me on my forehead and left.

I dragged myself to the bathroom. So weak, I fell twice getting there. I ran my bathwater so high, applying bleach into my water, scrubbing myself down, trying to get the feel of Paul off of me. As I lay in the tub, having flashbacks of what just happened to me, I cried. My face went underwater without holding my breath. I was ready to kill myself. I felt so disgusted. I then felt hands grabbing me, and it was Castile, who had just gotten off from work, asking, "Babe, what you are doing?"

As days and weeks went by, I decided to stay in and only leave out when it's a date with my boo, Castile. It only lasted for a month before I became bored at repeating the same thing over and over again—staying in the house, work, sex, and eating out. I called my friend up to see what she was up to for the weekend, and she told me that she didn't have any plans, but that night, which was Thursday, there was an event that was hosted by her boyfriend. There will be twelve male strippers performing for the ladies, and it will be big. I said to my friend, "I would love to go, but first, we have to do a little shopping."

I and my girlfriend met up, and we started picking out outfits for tonight and had our faces made up and our hair curled. We also had pedicure and manicure. "I can't wait until tonight," I said to my friend. Then we got a bite to eat, and we went our separate ways. We both said, "Kiss, kiss! See you at the event tonight," as we waved good-bye.

As I returned home, I ran a warm bubble bath and relaxed. After I completed my bath and finished drying off, I started rubbing lotion on my body. Staring at myself in the mirror brought back a lot of memories and thoughts on why he would mistreat me and cheat on me—all these finest, thick thighs, bootylicious, curve fitting, petite body? Not only that I was always good to him, but he also had a headstrong woman who handled her responsibilities as a woman, cooked, cleaned, and did any and everything for him until he got into the music business and started fucking over me, had sex with different women— almost the whole damn community. The secrets he kept hidden from me were all over the streets by words of mouths, chicken heads never keep their mouth close, and most of the time the side piece always try to let the main woman know what's going on, hoping he'll leave his home to be with her, but I still didn't believe it, because I loved my man. That goes to show you that no matter how beautiful and good of a woman that you are, a man is going to be a man. Sometimes, I have to think of myself, *Is being so good of a woman too good for a man? Or do I have to be a hoe to get treated right?* But anyway, let me dry my tears and stop reminiscing.

My phone started to ring. It was my friend saying she was parked outside, waiting. I told her to come in because I wasn't ready.

She said, "Bitch, you have to hurry up because my boyfriend has to be there in about an hour."

I said, "Okay, I just need thirty minutes, and the door is unlock, so come help yourself."

So my best friend and her boyfriend came in, and I got a knock at my bedroom door. It was just my best friend asking if she could go ahead and get dressed here instead of waiting until she got to the event.

I said, "Of course. The guest bedroom is upstairs to the right."

As I strapped on my heels—because my heels get put on the first before anything else—I began to take off my bathrobe that I had slipped on to unlock the door for my best friend. I then slipped my bra on, and I didn't have anything else to slip on but my dress because I wear no panties at all under my thin fitted dresses. I had to look at myself in the mirror, in love with myself. As I started slipping my earrings on, I saw hazel eyes staring at me. He was rubbing his chest and licking his lips. Boy, that turned me on, and seeing the print of his hard dick rising from his knees made my mind go blank, but my juices started flowing. Before I can even pull myself together, he had me on his face with his tongue.

Oh so deep into my . . . ooooooh, that feels so damn good. As he flipped me upside down, I began to suck on his dick, massaging his dick with my tongue and getting a mouthful. I then found myself riding Derek as if I had needed sex for a very long time. That's how good his dick was.

Afterward, Derek returned back to the living room while I took a quick PTA bath—pussy, titties, and armpits. While slipping on my dark-pink body-con dress, my BFF entered the room, staring at me all crazy and shit. As I stared back at her, I was saying in my mind, *I apologize.* I honestly was not, but all that came out from her mouth was, "Okay. It is time to go. Let's go."

As we entered the nice custom-design Range Rover, Derek stared out of the rearview mirror. I started looking out the back window to avoid looking into Derek's eyes. I thought guilt would run through me, knowing that I had just had sex with my BFF's boyfriend, but it didn't. I felt released, free, and full of energy.

As we arrived at the event center, there were so many people and long lines. Luckily, we were VIP with the main man himself, Mr. Derek. Music was playing and people were dancing and peeping the scene. I too was feeling the rhythm to the beat of the music. I started dancing and feeling myself, and my body started moving to the rhythm also. We had tequilas, back to back, enjoying ourselves.

Then I had to dismiss myself to the ladies' room to check my lipstick and make sure my hair was still on point. A white blond-headed woman, about six feet tall with thick Coke-shaped body, full thick lips, and long wavy hair, walked into the ladies' room with a drink in her hand, stared at me, and said, "I have been watching you all night. You so fucking hot," and she started kissing my neck, rubbing me on my legs. She moved her hands up my dress, massaging my pussy with her hands, fingering me just right, getting this pussy wet. *Ooooo.*

She licked my body all the way down, kissing, licking, and tongue-kissing my pussy. *Ooooo, yes.* As she gripped my ass and she worked her tongue into my vagina, I started playing with my nipples. I heard a door shut and lock, and I looked up when I felt another woman's hands around my nipples. As she started licking and sucking my nipples, I then started fingering her, and she started moaning. We all started moaning, having a threesome in the ladies' room. I can't even complain that felt good. Afterward, I returned to the party, and let's just say, each one of us women got what we had wanted.

As I was walking back to the VIP section, I felt a hand pull me behind some decorative hanging curtains. It was Victor. I responded, "Oh my god, what do you want?"

Victor started saying how he missed me and that he hadn't been able to stop thinking about me.

I told his ass he needed to stop thinking about me and go take care of all his kids and that wife of his. I was not cut out for any bullshit.

Victor stared at me and said, "I need you. I am in love with you."

I giggled at this and said, "Go fuck yourself," and I turned and walked away. I returned to my best friend's section, and we partied that whole night.

The next morning, I awakened to a hangover. I was too tired to get up, but I knew I had a lot of business to take care of. I also woke up hungry and thirsty, so I found myself having breakfast at the Maples Café. I ordered some chicken and waffles. While sitting at the table, eating my breakfast, a male approached me. He was dressed in a nice button-down dark-blue shirt, Peanut Butter belt, and faded denim jeans, and on his feet were Peanut Butter square-toe dress shoes. He was bald-headed, brown-skinned, mid-height muscular man. He was so damn fine.

"Excuse me, ma'am. Do you mind if I join you? I am lonely right now, and I don't want to eat alone," he said as he licked his lips.

In my mind, I said, *You won't ever have to worry about eating alone. OMG, I am going to have a meltdown.* I said to him, "Sure."

He then said, "Perry, Perry is my name, and you?"

I replied to him and said, "Sasha."

Perry told me a little about himself, and I told him about myself. We laughed, and for some reason, I felt as if I already knew him. Well, I had noticed time had gone by so quickly that I jumped up and said, "I have to go."

Perry asked if will he ever see me again, and I said, "No doubt." So I wrote my number on a napkin and excused myself so that I could go take care of some business before work tonight.

I did not finish running errands until two forty-five this afternoon. I got home two hours before and walked in to see Castile sitting at the dining room table, still in his scrubs. He wasn't supposed to be off work until another hour. He did not look so happy. I went over to kiss him, and he moved his head over. I then asked what was wrong.

Castile stood up and said that Ariel had come by the job looking for me, asking where his backstabbing hoe girlfriend was. "She had fucked my man, Derek, and I am going to beat that bitch."

Castile said at first that he had thought she was confused or high or maybe even drunk, but he could see it in my best friend Ariel's red watery eyes—her hurt, betrayal, and just pain written across her face. I had better had some powerful words to say to convince him that Ariel was not telling the truth. I started trying to lie about every bit of the truth Ariel had told, but while explaining, my front door was kicked open by Ariel, who ran and yelled toward me. I lost it. I started yelling, "I am sorry. I am so sorry, Ariel. I didn't mean to do it. He caught me off guard while I was in my room. I am sorry."

Ariel said to me in her hurtful, crying, crackling, angry tone, "Long as you live, bitch, you will never be my friend. You will always be that backstabbing hoe that you are, and do not call me anymore," and she went out the front door. I had fallen to the floor, hurt because I had betrayed my only best friend, and I was just as guilty as Derek was. I did not know what to do at that point.

I had forgotten Castile was home early. Standing behind me, he started to say, "I don't even care to ask when, how, and why it happened. I am going to get my stuff and leave. I don't want to see you anymore," and continued saying that his life is not going to be filled with lies, unfaithfulness, lust, or trash as he left.

I started crying, "No, Castile. Please don't leave me. I made a mistake, please." Tears rolled heavily down my face, and I started grabbing his hand, pulling him toward me. "Please forgive me," I cried. I could see Castile had tears in his eyes, and without saying anything, he put down his bags and gave me a hug and a kiss and said, "It's over," and he left along with all his belongings.

I cried myself that whole day, forgetting to go to work, even to call in. I felt afraid that I had no one to talk to or love me. I felt lost and lonely that I found myself on my sofa for days. I then heard my doorbell, and I moved very slowly to answer. It was my neighbor asking if everything was okay.

My mind was gone. But as days and nights passed by, I decided to get myself together. I returned to work. People stared at me and even had their backs turned as I walked through the hospital hall. I just wanted to run fast to my office because the halls looked so long. I gathered that everyone had heard what had happened. I just didn't know how much they knew. I was so stressed out. *Who am I? What have I done? What have I become?* I was not myself. I sat in my office, staring at a daze with the door shut, feeling lonely, like the whole world was against me. How selfish of me to not think of anyone else but myself and what dick I could ride and getting this pussy wet.

As I sat there thinking, I heard a loud knock at my office door, "Come in," I said. It was an intern student from Harvard who had introduced himself as Jared. As he handed me his paperwork, I went over rules, regulations, most of the duties he will be assigned to, and the learning steps he will take to become more knowledgeable of his practice.

We then took a tour around the hospital facility. While showing him around and meeting and greeting the staff, at the same time, I could feel, hear, and see the hatred, the cricket mouths, the eye rolling, and the gossip folks. I turned to continue the tour. I knew if I had noticed all the hot mess, Jared noticed it also. I was not feeling well at all.

Jared and I returned to the office. As we entered the office, Jared said, "Wow."

I turned and responded, "I know it may seem like it's a lot of work, but it is not. Once you start learning, you will find your way."

Jared started shaking his head. "No, no, no, ma'am. I was saying wow because of all the hatred and not-so-happy faces around here. What's going on?"

As I paused and stared, Jared waved his hand in front of my face. "Are you okay?" Jared asked.

"Yes. I mean, no," I replied as I started crying, saying, "I have nobody. I am hurting. It feels that I have no one to run to. I lost some good people in my life."

As tears poured down my face heavily, Jared stood up and went to lock the office door. "I am sorry, Ms. Lady. Sorry for your loss, and I don't know what you're going through, but don't let these people see you cry." He grabbed my hand, feeling sorry for me, not even knowing that I was not the person he should feel sorry for and I caused myself to go through this.

Jared had moved even closer to me as his hand massaged my shoulders then moved slowly to my lower back. His strong, manly hands felt so good and hit all the right spots as Jared went even farther to my inner thighs. Before I could even think about what was going on, I found his dick inside of me, fucking me on top of my office desk. His dick was so huge and so good. At that time, I didn't care who he was. I needed that, and my energy levels shot right up. As Jared flipped me around, hitting me from behind and sideways, using his tongue to massage the inner muscles of my pussy, I said, "Yes, yes. Fuck me." I sucked his dick while he massaged my head as I massaged his dick with the back of my throat. That made my whole work day.

At night, I started having weird dreams about bad things—me lying in the streets, sometimes blood pouring down my face, and about a man with no face. The dreams were so weird it felt as if I were present in it, but I couldn't see myself. It was as if the dream never had an ending, and it's funny because I never ever dreamed of how the dream even got started. I woke up yelling, "Are you okay?" but no one else was there but my empty room and pitch-black darkness.

These sleepless nights got me scared, so I called my best friend Ariel to see if she would talk to me or come over, and I also wanted to let her know how sorry I was and I missed having her around.

She answered the phone, and I said, "Hi. Give me just a little of your time."

She said to me, "Whore, you got two seconds."

I told her I needed her, that I was so lost, and that I was sorry.

She then told me, "Bitch, I would not care if you don't ever find your way. I don't care, bitch, if you fall off a fucking cliff. Don't you ever call my fucking phone, and I still haven't made up my mind if I should kick your ass or not," and she hung up.

I knew I stepped out of line. My guilt side played it over and over in my head, or was it that I just missed my best friend? I sat there thinking, *Who else could I call?* Victor came across my mind—the warmth of his muscled arms, hard pillow top chest, and his scent and aroma that will have you never wanting to let go. I picked up the phone and called him next. The phone rang, rang, and rang, and the voice mail picked up. I hung up and called his phone again.

"Hello," a woman said, and I hung up. That night, I just stayed up until my mind dozed off on its own.

The next morning, I was awakened by loud noises coming from outside and the sound of police car sirens. I opened the curtains and looked down. There were so many people out front I could not see what was going on, so I slipped on some pajamas and grabbed my robe and went out the door to see what was going on. As I started squeezing through the crowd, I noticed some people staring at me, shaking their heads. I then noticed that it was my car. The windows were bust out, the seats cut up, and the tires on flat. There were dents on every side and scratches from front to back, and on my window was written in red paint "Hoe, if you only knew what is coming to you," and on another window, it had "You fuck the wrong husband," and one on the front window said, "Cliqueless hoe."

The cops asked if I was the owner, and I said yes. As the cops started asking questions, my mind went blank and I did not hear a word. *My Range Rover, my vehicle I had paid hard, earned money for, who would do this?* I asked myself, *Why? And how come no one heard anything?* I started yelling out, "How come no one heard anything? How come? I know somebody saw something!"

The cops started yelling for me to calm down, and the looks on their faces were as if they thought something was wrong with me. They took me down to the station for questioning. They questioned me about having any mental issues, about my sex life, about having any enemies, about my parents, friends, and all kind of things. Then they handed me a card and said that if I remember anything, to give them a call. This was after I had told the stupid motherfuckers that nothing happened and that I was home alone asleep. I can't believe those sorry-ass cops.

It was noon when I left the police station, and at five o'clock, I had to go to work. My whole life felt not just tilted to the side but flipped completely over. I needed to take a run. I needed to free and clear my mind, for I actually cracked the fuck up. I returned home and put on some exercise clothing. I didn't jog—I ran and ran. I felt the sweat pouring off me. My shirt was so wet it stuck to my skin. I took a rest at a park bench, and I started crying. I cried and cried and asked myself, *Why me? What am I going through? And what have I done?*

A woman approached me, an old Caucasian woman in her early or late sixties, and she asked if I was okay, and I just stared at her as a heavy flow of tears rolled down my face. As I just stared at the woman, the woman sat on the side of me and rubbed my back and said, "I don't know you, but whatever you're going through, honey, it's heavy, dark, and it's bad, and if you don't pull yourself together, it's going to get ugly."

I looked up at her, and she said, "If you don't pull yourself together, it will get out of hand. You have a cloud over you, and you don't want it to pour the wrong things down. It could be very bad, and I am not talking about no lightning, ice, or water. It's hell. It's death, child. Pull yourself together, or it will rip you apart, especially when you don't fix your ways, child, and whatever you are doing out here in this world, you better stop before it stops you."

I asked the lady who she was, and she just got up and left. I feared of being alone. I feared of myself. *Why are bad things happening to me? And why does the whole world feel like it's against me? Who have I become?*

I returned to my house and took a long shower, got out, and got dressed for work. The old lady was running through my head. I caught a taxi to work. Once I got to work, I checked the workers' paperwork, asked if there were any problems or concerns, checked schedules, and told the staff that if anyone needed me, just knock at my office or call the office phone and that I'll be in there doing paperwork. I then went straight into my office and locked the door. I sat there thinking and tried putting the puzzle pieces together— of the things I did wrong, whom I have hurt, who would want to harm me in any kind of way, and why make my life miserable.

Have I done anything that bad to make the world hate me? I started writing things down about what I have done. I started writing names of all the men I have been involved with and all the women whom I had a falling-out with or they fell out with me. I wondered if my grandmother has the same number. I haven't spoken to her in years, and I actually barely knew her. I met her at my mother's funeral. My mom died years ago in a car crash. I crawled out the backseat and was taken to the hospital by a homeless lady whom, in my teenage years, I found out about and gave half of the money to—money that my mother had left me. I called the number. I remembered. But there was no answer, not even a ringtone. The number was disconnected.

I then got on the computer and looked her up. I wrote the address down. *Tomorrow I will visit.* As I started thinking of all the things I could share with my grandmother and that someone can finally hear and listen to my cries and can probably give me advice on what I needed to do, someone knocked on my office door. "Come in," I said. It was Nurse Kimberly, who said she had needed to talk to me. She said that she noticed a distance between the staff and me and that she heard all sorts of things and that some people are still there for others no matter how wrong they are or how many things they have done in their life, and she just wanted to let me know, if I needed anything, that I still have her. How sweet.

The next morning, around two o'clock in the morning, I closed up my office and caught a ride with Kimberly to my house. That morning, I got some sleep, and that noon, I decided to gather some things and catch a taxi to visit my grandmother's house. She stayed two hours away in Kookiville. I was so excited. I couldn't wait to meet her.

As I traveled to Kookiville, I stared out at the beautiful sky and the beautiful dollhouse-shaped houses, but you know what, I could not remember half of my childhood, no memories at all. I just had one picture of my beautiful mother, and I remember the story that the homeless lady, Mrs. Jessie, told me. Mrs. Jessie stayed by my bedside while I was in the hospital, even though they wanted to throw her out. A detective told me they saw care in her eyes, and they told her that she could stay, and that she did, all the way up until I was eighteen, old enough to move out on my own. Mrs. Jessie and I hadn't spoken in a while because I asked about my real mother and because I wanted to know more, so we had an argument. The towns built the lady a home and gave her a family, which was me. I never did know why my grandmother or any relative didn't take me in, and I never did ask, even when I saw my grandmother at the funeral.

As I arrived at the front of my grandmother's house, I walked up the high stairs, and I knocked at her door. I was so excited to see my mom's mother. As I rubbed both my hands together, nervous and happy at the same time, the door slowly opened, and this beautiful old lady stood there, staring at me but not in a good way. She said to me, "You look just like him," and she started shedding tears.

I said, "Oh, Grandmother, don't cry. Is he, Grandmother, my father?"

She shut the door on my face and said, "Just go."

I started knocking at the door. "Grandmother, I need you! I need you, Grandmother!" I started shouting.

That's when Grandmother opened the door and said, "Come in, child."

She sat down, and I sat beside her, and she looked at me with her watery eyes as she rubbed my hair and then gave me a hug, saying she was so sorry and that she lived with guilt every day about what happened to my mother. I didn't quite understand.

"It was just a car wreck, Grandmother. It was an accident. It was not your fault," I said as I hugged my grandmother.

My grandmother said, "Okay, enough with me now. What brings you here?"

I then said to her, "Grandmother, I have been through a lot. I did a lot of bad things, and I have run off good people in my life. I need someone to talk to, and I am losing it."

My grandmother looked at me and said, "My ears are all yours."

As I started talking, my grandmother listened, and then she cut me off and said, "You just like your mother. Get out! You a slut, and not only do you remind me of that low-life bastard. You have your whore of a mother. You sick! Get out! Get out!" My grandmother shouted.

"I don't understand."

Grandmother said, "What's going on with you? You whore! Get out my house!"

As tears rolled down my eyes, I left. I saw the look on her face. It was mean, hurtful, and evil at the same time.

I started walking down the streets, crying, and I called a taxi to pick me up. I then really needed a shoulder to cry on, so I had the taxi bring me to the only mother I knew—Mrs. Jessie.

As I pulled up to the home I was raised in, I slowly dragged myself to the door, hoping that she wouldn't flip on me like my grandmother did. I rang her doorbell, and Mrs. Jessie opened it and started crying and grabbed hold of me, hugging me, saying, "I looked all over for you. I called different numbers. I thought you forgot about me." Mrs. Jessie looked at my face and said, "Sasha, what is the matter, my girl?" I just hugged her even tighter as I cried.

I finally calmed down and was able to tell her everything, and she cried and held my hand the whole time. She listened. I needed that. Mrs. Jessie then told me that my mother's car wreck wasn't an accident, that the car that hit and ran, flipping my mother's car over, was my grandmother—my mother's mom.

She said, "I witnessed it. I saw your grandmother run straight into her. I saw your grandmother get out and look straight at your mother's flipped car. I saw where she just looked down at your mother's hand as she reached out to her mom for help, and she just left her there to die. I didn't want your mother's killer to notice me, an old homeless woman. I didn't want your grandmother to kill me next, so I lay there in front of the abandoned building as I peeped from under my dusty blanket."

Tears rolled down my eyes so heavily that I wet Mrs. Jessie's shirt. As I listened to Mrs. Jessie continue to tell what happened, I cried and cried. Mrs. Jessie then said that my grandmother got into her wrecked car and drove off. Mrs. Jessie then tiptoed over to the flaming car and reached out to my mother, who had no pulse. She noticed a small hand sticking out from under a pink-and-purple blanket. "It was you, Sasha. I grabbed you and took you to the hospital. You never crawled out. I just told you that story so that you won't be hurt by the evilness you grandmother did."

My whole face was red and wet. "But why would she do such thing? Why?" I cried.

As Mrs. Jessie looked at me, she grabbed my hand and said, "Your grandmother's fiancé is your biological father."

I cried even harder.

She said, "Your mother was messing with a man whom she had no idea was engaged to her mother. Your mom never met him. He said he never knew that your mother was the daughter of his fiancée. He was having an affair with another woman, a busy woman, which was your mother. They only saw each other at night, until your grandmother gave a party for her forty-eighth birthday, and that's when everything blew up, your father said. That's when everyone found out about what was going on. Your father is locked up at the pen. He lost it when he found out and took the blame for what happened to your mother. He didn't even know about you."

I looked at Mrs. Jessie and asked how she knew.

She said to me, "I didn't just take the state money for nothing. I graduated from college, earned my degree, and joined the investigation department. I dug deep into this murder, and when your father walked into the office a year later and turned his self in after your grandmother was constantly being questioned, the case was dropped, but I questioned your dad, and after he gave in, I sent the case to be reopened. But the case is still pending, and I guess he needs to sit there for a while to think that if he had just stuck with only one woman, then neither would be hurt. Your grandmother will suffer for a very long time because no mother could ever live right when murdering her own child that she bore. Your grandmother lost herself that same night. She walked away from that burning car with her daughter inside, not knowing about you until years later after being under investigation for so long."

That's what my grandmother meant when she said I look just like him. I started thinking of all the married men I have slept with and all the other men I lay with. I couldn't be my mother, and I knew all the wrongdoings I have done, but my mother did not. *I am a bad person. Oh my god.* I cried myself to sleep, and the next morning, I awoken with Mrs. Jessie right by my side.

Mrs. Jessie and I went out for breakfast the next day. I kept thinking in my head of the hurt heart and the lost daughter and the broken little girl, which was me, who had no idea that life would turn out the way that it did. I called in to work for a week, and I stayed a week out there with Mrs. Jessie to clear my head and soak up some of my hurt and stress. I visited my mother's grave, and I and Mrs. Jessie reconciled. As a matter of fact, the love was still there, and I wasn't looked at any different by her.

I returned home the very next day. I did a lot of house cleaning and just redecorated a little. I cooked and cleaned, and that afternoon, I went to purchase a brand-new Rover. I had to get my head together. I decided to relax for the rest of the day. I watched television and ate ice cream all day. It felt as if I were starting all over in a world by myself. Well, in life we either live and learn or we live and be nothing, just a body that's not accounted for, that doesn't even matter.

Later that night, I noticed my computer flashing, and I went to check it out. It was an e-mail flyer for a party at the Bonkays Club. That was a popular club out here. The sender was unknown.

I don't know about that one. I could get dressed and step out. Maybe I could meet new friends. I jumped off the sofa. *Why not? I am not about to stress myself or wear off the pillows on my couch, turning old before my age.* I opened the door to what every woman dreams of—a walk-in closet with everything in it, from handbags, designer blouses, dresses, skirts, pants, designer shoes, you name it, and it was all here. The only hard thing about it was figuring out what to wear. *Uh-oh, bingo.*

I ran my hot bubble bath, poured myself a little champagne, and relaxed. I slipped on my all-black lace jumpsuit with my black red-bottomed stilettos and my red clutch and colored my full lips red. Sometimes, I have to say, I made myself hot. I had an attitude, and I wore it well. I thought highly of myself but way too highly. I didn't know how I was starting to look to the public's eyes. Oh well, ladies need to give themselves props, and for the ones who don't got it, don't judge the ones who do. You either get it or buy it or shut up, and for the ladies that have it, accept it. Embrace your beauty. People's mind is going to wonder anyway, whether you have clothes on or not, whether you have booty or not, whether your pussy stinks or not. Men are still going to wonder. Men are always sniffing around.

I woke up tied to a bed rail in a room with mirrors all around. I couldn't remember how I got here, here in a dark room. There's no one or anything in here but a bed and myself. Even looking through the mirrors, I can see nothing but me. I have been stripped down to my panties and bra.

"Hello!" I yelled. "Is anybody here?" *This shit is a little weird,* I thought to myself.

The door opened, and a sexy blond muscular man wearing a mask walked in, and I saw that he was a white male.

"I don't remember meeting you," I said.

The man replied, "Oh, I remember meeting you." He walked by the bed, pulling my head back by my hair as if he were about to kiss me. Instead he whispered in my ear, "I am going to fuck you up."

I said as I laughed, "That's what I want. That's what I like. Foreplay is a turn on, baby."

The masked man walked out as he gave a weird look, and he left the room, closing the door.

"Okay, you sexy-ass motherfucker, you taking too damn long to handle your business. Let's get this show on the road." I noticed time was ticking. An hour had passed, and another thirty minutes went by. I started yelling, "Okay, white man. Come untie me. I am not in the mood anymore."

There was no response. My heart started beating fast. I was shaking, trying to untie myself, but the cuff wasn't coming loose. I started yelling louder, "Okay, motherfucker, untie me!" There was no one responding back but the echoes of my voice. "What the hell is going on?" I yelled. I kept yelling until I had no voice to yell anymore. Instead, I cried myself to sleep.

The next morning, I had awakened naked, but this time, only both legs were tied off at the foot of the bed and both hands were at the headrails. I noticed the masked man walking toward me with his hands behind his back as he approached the bed, climbing in between my legs.

I asked, "Who are you? What do you want? And why are you doing this?"

The masked man said, "I want to see your face expressions."

"What face expressions?" I asked, and the man did not reply. Instead he rubbed my hair as he pulled a huge black dildo from behind his back, rubbing my thighs up to my belly button, pressing against my nipples in a circular motion.

I started crying, "Please stop. I have never done you anything. Please let me go."

The masked man never said a word. The only sound that could be heard was the sound of me screaming while that man fucked me, shoving the huge dildo up into my pussy as he watched me make painful face expressions and as I balled my hands so tightly. The masked man worked the dildo into my vagina for two hours until I passed out.

I woke up hours later, but only this time, I was tied right in front of the mirror in my panties and bra. I started screaming, "What the fuck is going on? Somebody help me!" I cried and cried, and I even tried yanking the handcuffs and chains loose, but they did not budge. I didn't have anyone to yell to, and there was no one that could hear my cries. The room was empty. I couldn't maneuver myself around to the other section of the room. I could only see myself in the mirror. I stared at my broken self as tears rolled down my eyes. I even thought, *What have I done? Whom have I become? What does this person want from me?*

I sat there, thinking over and over again of all the wrongful things I did and the bad dreams I had, and I even thought about the last words that the old lady said to me at the park. I just couldn't narrow it down to who was this masked man that was doing this to me.

The man with the mask returned into the dark, empty, echoing room, where I just stared off into a mirror, which the masked man cleaned every chance he got to make sure that my image was not smeared or blurred out by fogged-up mirror. He felt that I had needed to think about everything I had done and everyone I had hurt and to see the pitiful woman that I was—a pretty brown-skinned woman with an ugly image that I couldn't even see or notice because the thought of my mind being made up and my ego so high that no one can tell me anything different. But this time, not only was I told, but I also learned, faced, and knew how it felt to hurt.

"Like I did when I heard my husband call your name while we are in the middle of sex. As I thought about that moment, I started picturing it, seeing his and your face in my head, God, it made me even madder," the masked man said as he started punching me and slapping me around, and before he could realize it, he saw blood.

He stopped. He had to control himself. *I can't let this coldhearted person get the best of me.*

I was knocked out on the floor. The masked man reached to feel to see if I still had a pulse, and I did. The masked man decided to leave the room, but he came back two seconds later, screaming, "Why? Why did you have to hurt me, Sasha? Why? Why can't you be normal like everyone else? Why can't you think of others? What do you get out of it, Sasha?" the masked man asked. "I mean, do you like a lot of sex, bitch? Huh? Do you?" As his anger kept building up and building up, he asked, "Do you?" He grabbed me by my hair, loosening the chains, flipping me over as he said, "You like sex so much, I'll give you just that."

He shoved his dick into my rear end. All that could be heard was my heavy tears as they hit the puddle of water on the floor that was made from my cries. My face was so swollen that I couldn't open my mouth to scream even if I wanted to.

An hour later, the masked man crawled off me and stood up and said, "That would hold your ass still." He started facing the mirror and talking to himself, "I won't ever be hurt again. Remember, I told you that, boy. Remember, I said that, and I meant that. I am his protector. I told him 'I do' at the altar, and this is how he repays me? Thought just drives me crazy. Am I crazy?" he asked himself. "No, no, no. I can't be. I think I am just mad as hell. I just want to protect him. He is my husband, my love, and no one will take him from me, not like my mother took my first lover. Even though my first love had me in pain and feeling loved at the same time, but my love for my husband has me feeling loved and happy at the same time, but here it is, years later, I am feeling hurt again, not love. Could it be I am losing him to her?"

He glanced at me through the mirror. I could see this guy talking to himself as if he has lost it or just plain crazy. The masked man started wiping his tears as he turned to face me, and he said, "Not this time, bitch. You won't take him from me." He stood straight up, and he walked off and repeatedly said, "Not this time."

Why? Why do women just give themselves up to any and every guy that they see? Why do they continue to have sexual relations with a married man? Why do women get this I-look-good and I-can-have-anybody-I-want type of attitude? Why are most women so coldhearted that they look to hurt the next woman for no reason instead of building each other up? How come women don't see that the reason they're in the same boat and haven't been proposed to is because they're chasing or sleeping with some guy that is already taken? Most women get comfortable and feel complete by someone else's man because of the gifts and the materialistic things that the man buys for them or the good sex that is made to them and not thinking of why he hasn't left his wife or not noticing yet that they will never be together besides in sex. Days, months, and years later, the relationship or the love triangle hasn't gone anywhere.

Women create that image without noticing because they are blinded by the lust, and they confuse the meaning of the definition of *love* or *being in love* as "I care for you" and just being a sex partner. Loving someone is deep, having their best interest in mind, a spiritual connection. When they say "I care for you" but don't love you, it means, "I have interest in you. I like your company. You're just a buddy, nothing more." Most bitches go crazy when they find out that men don't love them, yet it was never sad he did. The woman just took it that way, or if he said it, his action told otherwise.

Sex can make anyone do the wrong thing, cheat, lose their mind, and get their asses beaten, like Sasha, this Ms. Queen Bitch who slept with men left to right, right to left, but had sex with the wrong husband—my husband, the man that I love. Little Ms. Pretty Sasha got herself an image of being a hoe, using her beauty to attract a handsome, respectable man and having him at the palms of her hands, being treated like a queen, and being a woman that she could have been other than a community hoe everybody had a piece of. Now who's going to want her? Little Ms. Sasha walked through the club in her nice fur outfit, with her banging body, head so high, thinking everybody wanted her, but little did she know that people has started gossiping and planning who could get her panties next, yet she thought she was popular because folks were speaking, giving her hugs, buying her drinks, just being friendly, hoping they would get picked next to fuck Sasha. A flower can bloom so beautiful but die so easily that a drip of water won't save it.

The man in the mask brought in some food to Sasha and made her eat it out of a bowl. He felt that she carried herself like a dog in heat that she might as well get treated like one. Even her water, she drank that out of a bowl too.

Levy is my name. I am a fair, loyal, and friendly person until you fuck with the love of my life—the one I invest all my time, money, and life into, and I am damned if I let another woman or man come in to take my property, and if you touch it, hoe, you trespassing. When I said 'Until death do us part,' I meant that, but only it won't be his death or mine. It will be of the bitch who had no reason intruding in my marriage because she wanted to run the streets being a hoe. When they say when married you become one, in my eyes, you fuck with him. That means you fucking with me, and I will come for you, because he is going nowhere. I will eliminate the problem before I let this marriage end by a hoe.

I am an emotional person, but when my heart is heavy and hurt, and when these coldhearted people start doing things to hurt another human being with no care in the world, you have people like me that can change in a split second and mess a hoe up. People say you never know who a person really is. That's true, but people change every day. That best friend becomes your enemy because they stab you in the back, sleep with your man or woman, gossip all the time, pull you down with them, don't like to see you happy, don't motivate you in any kind of way, are always at your house and never at work, make faces and ready to fight you, always mug others, constantly lie, always loud in public, and has been in the same boat since day 1.

The lovers that put all time in the world with his or her spouse become the murder of them, and they pull that gun on his or her, committing suicide or going to jail so that no one can have them or no one will leave, but till death do us part. The man that you trust in your home, the man that you women fall in love with, become the molester of your child, but you are so blinded by that false devilish love that the attention of the importance and the love of your child is forgotten about because you're trying to please that man that you really didn't know anything about or the way your child cries out to you without shedding a tear because a child knows no better or he just tires of the abuse and just gives up.

I was just tired, but my mother paid me no mind. She never saw her lover was my abuser, and I was only five years of age. My cries, no one heard, not even my mother. I would go and tap her on the shoulder and hug her around her neck, letting her know that I needed her. "I am hurting, Mom." But still she brushed me off, just laughing away with that monster, who gave her the finest things, the materialistic things that caught her eyes, the things that made her forget about me.

I never forgave my mother what had happened to me. I tried, but it constantly played over and over in my head. His face was what I saw. Later in life, I was twelve years of age when my mother's monster lover became the first man I fell in love with.

One day, we were having dinner, and I decide to tell my mother about my lover. That man stood up and slapped me out of my seat to the floor, and all I could see was my mother's face turning so red as if the devil himself took over her body, and all I remember was my mother's monster lover, who had become the love of my life, falling to the floor. She had done stabbed him. Her action was so quick she didn't have time to think. But me, being five years of age, she never took the time to listen, to check on me, to even know that I needed her more than anything. Her actions were not as quick as they were when I told her who my lover was. I think she was mad at her monster lover for loving two people at the same time and not because I was her child, who was crying out for help, and she never heard a sound because her mind was focused on making him happy, and her eyes were blinded by the false devilish love and materialistic things.

Now my mother sat in jail, awaiting parole for the third time. That monster that became my lover was buried the next weekend.

I always told myself I will not get hurt again, and I meant that, and that's why I did what I had to do to eliminate the problem, and Sasha was my problem. I barely knew the bitch. Word on the street was she was a hoe and that she'd been messing with people's husbands, and one having to be mine, and I found out that one myself. While making love, his ass called me her name. I did a little investigating, and I dug the hoe right up. Now the hoe won't bother anyone else, and the problem is solved. My husband is Jared, and I am his protector. You fuck with him, and the masked man will fuck with you. I will not hurt again.

The masked man decided that he was tired of having Sasha around. The more he kept her in his mind, the angrier he had become. He returned into the room, but only this time, he made Sasha caress herself in front of him and play with herself until she cum, and when his hormones started racing and his dick arouse, he forced Sasha to give him oral sex. Her jaws were so swollen she could barely suck it right, but he made sure she did. When her teeth scraped the skin of his dick, he slapped her, and he made it clear to her that if she bit down or did anything stupid, he would cut her head off without having to think twice about it.

Sasha gave him exactly what he had wanted. Afterward, he decided to take Sasha's life by stabbing her and letting her bleed to her death. Sasha felt her blood just running down her body. She felt the pool of her own blood so heavy and thick. She felt her tears roll off her swollen, painful cheeks. She reached for the person in the mirror, whispering at herself, saying, "I am sorry for what I have done." The person in the mirror was the image of herself that she destroyed. She watched herself fade away through the mirror as she died slowly.

Sasha was found dead months later in an abandoned house in the woods, chained to a bed in an upward position, as if she had been staring at herself before she took her last breath, the cops said. Her body looked as if it were drained.

There are signs of heartless people everywhere. Humans have a mind of their own. They're like a computer chip. The mind stores memory, deletes memory, and catches virus all the time. Can't you tell? The mood swings, attitudes, and the people that you hang around or accept in your life are what the memory feeds on. The company you keep will make you or break you and could even affect the ones that you love. Your image is everything.

"If only I could imagine what Sasha went through," Sasha ex-best friend Ariel said. "I stopped talking to her and ignored her, and she needed my help. Sasha was in trouble, and I couldn't even save her. I let a man come between my relationship with best friend." Ariel cried and cried as she looked at the photos that the police had shown to her. "It's all my fault. I should have been there for her."

Sasha's friend cried so much the police barely could question her anymore that day, but they could tell from everyone else that they had questioned that Sasha was not everyone's friend and that Sasha had developed an image that her death didn't leave everyone in tears but only her friend and the mother that raised her. Sasha was a beautiful woman who slept around with married men, crazy men, friends' boyfriends, and women. She was just a good girl who decided to experience the single life, party, have fun, sex, and just be happy (at least that's what she thought) but made enemies from every angle, not focusing on others, not thinking that she could be hurting and breaking up happy homes by messing with theses married men.

Folks are blinded by what they call a spotlight. You give them a little attention, they begin to think they are superstars.

"She was a good friend, and then later, she became a whole different woman. I felt I didn't even know her anymore," Ariel said, looking up at the police as she cried. "I should have questioned her and tried to figure out what she was going through, but instead, I wanted to beat her. I wanted to beat her so bad because she had slept with my man—a man who made that choice to sleep with my friend, a man that could have said no, a man that should have told me about it instead of keeping it from me, a man that has no excuse for having sex with another woman knowing he has a woman, a man who had a pitiful excuse for why he did it, and a man I let go of." Ariel cried. The cops could see how hurt she was.

This is a cold, cold world we live in, and it's up to the people to make it whole. There are people leaving it day by day. Children, men, and women are disappearing, and there are abuse and cries that no one could hear or save. People commit suicide because they are going through some things. The guidance that is not being taught to the people that need it the most, the love that is not present at the right time, all these things that people don't give to one another, like love, car, motivation, and attention, 'cause of the way people act, if we put all these things together, the people in this world would be a lot better, and they would know how to come together instead of being separate.

The police questioned the staff at the hospital where Sasha had worked, as well as the wives, girlfriends, cheating husbands, and boyfriends, about Sasha, trying to narrow her death down. They wanted to know who the murderer was, but if the cops had to choose, it would have been all of them. Nothing good came out of those people's mouths. One guy seemed silent and really didn't have much to say, but he had just known of Sasha for a short period of time because he had just started working at the hospital. The police even asked if he had any type of relations with Ms. Sasha, and Jared replied, "No, not at all. I am married to my husband, and I don't have any relations with women."

As Jared told that to the police, the police noticed the shaking of his hands, and Jared not once made eye contact with the officers.

The police asked again, "So you had no relations with Ms. Sasha?"

Jared yelled, "No! I am a gay man, okay! A gay man that is happily married!"

The cops didn't like the actions of Jared, so they made sure they kept a close eye on him. They wanted to know more about him.

The next day, Jared's husband was called to the police station for questioning, just to be fair with questioning everyone and making sure no one was skipped, not even the people in same-sex relationships.

The police asked Jared's husband to state his name and the husband said, "Levy is my name, and I have no knowledge of anyone's death. I don't know the hoe personally. I only heard of her, and I could care less about her from what she stands for."

Pretty much, Levy told the cops what they wanted to hear, but one investigator by the name of Ernie didn't buy Levy's talk at all because he knew that something was not right. Investigator Ernie asked Levy, "Have you ever been outside your marriage?"

Levy got quiet and stared at the investigator with this crazy, mad-killer look as if he were possessed, and the investigator said, "Answer the question, Levy."

Levy asked the investigator, "Have you ever been outside your marriage, Ernie?"

Ernie looked at Levy and said, "Answer the question."

Levy then leaned back in the chair and said, "I told the preacher 'I do,' and I was wedded with the one I love, and no one can make me feel any different about my husband, so to answer your question, no, I have not been outside my marriage."

Levy was released from questioning because they did not have anything on him and no evidence at all, nothing but the body of Sasha, a mirror with her handprints, and the chains that she was tied to, along with a bloody mattress.

Jared had no idea why the police would question Levy. He didn't even know Sasha, at least that's what he thought. Jared was nerved up because of Sasha's death. He was pacing up and down the house as Levy sat at the dinner table, just watching him.

"Oh, just stop it. Stop the pacing, and sit down and eat."

Jared still paced up and down and didn't eat and barely slept through the night.

The next morning, Levy was sitting in the rocking chair, just rocking away. Jared was awakened by the sound of the squeaking coming from the chair rocking back and forth.

"Did you love her?" Levy asked.

"What?" Jared asked.

"You heard me!" Levy yelled. "Did you love her?"

Jared replied to Levy, "Baby, no. I barely knew her."

"Are you lying to me?" Levy asked.

"No, I wouldn't lie to you," Jared said to him.

Levy got up and started walking around the room, staring at Jared, "Did you ever sleep with her?"

"No, Levy!" Jared yelled. "You know me better than that."

Levy started laughing. "I do?" Levy asked. "Do I know you, Jared?" Levy started laughing again, and he said to Jared, "I thought you love me. I thought we were the best of friends. I thought we were happy. I thought nothing, no one, can pull us apart. I thought we had an honest marriage."

Jared sat up in bed and said, "We do."

Levy yelled, "Shut up! Just shut up, Jared! You love me." Levy crawled into bed toward Jared and said again, "You love me."

Jared got kind of scared because he'd never known Levy to act that way. He never saw him to seem as if he were possessed. Jared replied back, saying, "I love you with all my heart and soul, honey."

As he leaned over to kiss Levy, Levy slapped him. "I can't believe you. You slept with that hoe in her office. You made love to her, and you shared the passion that you shared with me."

Jared looked puzzled, and no words came out of his mouth. Levy got up and stumbled out of the room. Jared didn't know what to do or say. He just sat there. Levy came back in the room and said to Jared as he wiped his tears, "I said 'I do and until death do us part.' That's the only way. I mean, that's the only way we will depart from each other, and I mean every word of it. Now I am going to the grocery store and pick up some things to cook later. Do you need anything while I am out?"

Jared just looked at Levy and shook his head no. Levy grabbed his coat and left out. Jared started thinking that Levy had something to do with the murder of Sasha, because he saw a different side of his husband that he had never seen before. Jared got up and started searching the house for any signs of blood or something left behind that could lead to the murder.

Jared didn't find anything around the house. He sat on the sofa, just thinking who has his husband become, if he was even a murderer. Jared flipped through planners, looked through drawers, briefcases, and coat pockets, but there was no sign of murder. Jared spotted a weird-looking mask, but nothing else.

Levy had returned from the grocery store. He walked in, jolly and singing out loud.

This is not whom I had married, Jared thought.

Levy said, "I am cooking roast beef, mashed potatoes, and green beans, and red wine." He was hoping Jared would reply about the meal he was getting ready to prepare, but instead, Jared just stared at him. "Umm, hello, honey. Doesn't it sound good?" Levy said.

Jared then said, "Yeah, honey, it does. Can't wait to have some."

Levy got quiet and peeped his head from the kitchen, "Umm, Jared, honey, you usually in the kitchen hugging me, kissing me, helping me cut up the bell pepper, onions, and stuff the roast. What's going on?"

Jared said, "I don't feel good. I just need to go for a walk," and he got up and left out the door.

Levy continued cooking in the kitchen, preparing their meal for that day. Jared was walking in the park, not thinking of Levy, but thinking of the last time he had seen Sasha and how he had sex with her, knowing that something was wrong, knowing that the staff talked about how easy she was to get, and he took advantage of that poor woman. Jared felt guilt, and he kept seeing that image of him having sex with her—her facial expressions that she had made, and he could still feel her thighs pressing against his face and still could taste her juices on his tongue.

Jared saw Sasha in his head. Jared started crying, saying out loud, "What have I done?" His guilt filled his head up. It had him tripping in the park. Jared sat down on the bench to cool off and calm down. A little old lady was already sitting there, and she leaned over and said, "It's not good to hurt people. I told her the same thing, you know."

Jared said, "Excuse me? Who are you? And what are you talking about?"

The old woman got up and said, "The eyes sees everything even when you think no one is watching," and she got up and walked away.

Jared ran behind the old lady, grabbing her by her old, dusty coat. The lady said to him, "Let go of me."

Jared kept saying, "What do you know? What are you talking about?"

The old lady started screaming loudly, "Let go of me! Let go of me!"

People in the park started running over to help, thinking that Jared was trying to mug the old lady. The people were grabbing Jared and started pushing him around.

"Wait!" Jared said. "I was just questioning her, not harming her."

The people scattered, and by then, the old lady was gone.

He looked all around, but there was no sign of her. While Jared was walking back home, a police car pulled in front of him, and the detective was saying that they got a call reporting that he was trying to rob an old lady and that he had a nervous breakdown.

Jared said to the detective, "No, I wasn't trying to rob anyone. That the old lady said something to me, so I followed her, trying to find out what she meant."

The detective said, "Was it about Sasha's murder?"

Jared paused and said, "No," and he walked off.

Jared returned home, and Levy had the lights off, with candlelight and dinner and wine on the table, and he had on a red lingerie and a wig of the same color and length as Sasha's hair. He even had a brown-skinned mask that he had put on as he walked toward Jared, saying, "This is what you like. Is this what you want?"

Jared pushed Levy. "Get the hell away from me! Who the hell are you?" Jared asked. "You starting to act really weird, and you scaring the fuck out of me."

Levy kept pushing up on Jared. "I am your husband. I am the one you said you love. I am the one you said until death do us part." Levy slowed his voice down and said, "I am Sasha."

Jared looked at Levy and started backing up. "Who are you? And what have you done?"

Levy took off the mask, and Jared saw the tears rolling the down Levy's face as he said, "I told myself that I won't hurt anymore and that no one can take you from me. I told her the same thing. She didn't care about my feelings. She just thought about herself."

Jared opened the front door and left. He ran so fast to the hospital where he worked and just sat in Sasha's office. Sasha's pictures were still up, and Jared just sat there, thinking, trying to get his mind together. He started hearing someone crying. He opened the sliding door to the other side of Sasha's office. It was a woman. She said she was Sasha's friend Ariel. "She cried out to me, and I didn't help her."

Jared went over and hugged her and said, "I think I know who did this."

Ariel got quiet as she lifted her head off Jared's shoulder. "Who?" Ariel said. "Was it you?" she asked.

Jared said, "No, I think it was my husband."

Ariel got up and ran for the phone to call the police, but Jared snatched the cord out the wall. Ariel started running for the door, but Jared caught her and put his hand over her mouth, saying, "Wait, wait. It wasn't me. I didn't have anything to do with her death. I am just finding this out tonight, and I don't have enough evidence to prove he did it." He moved his hand from her mouth, putting them on his hips.

"Well, how do you know your husband did it? And why would he kill Sasha?" she asked. Jared was quiet, and Ariel looked up at Jared. "You, you bastard. You seduced her. You had sex with Sasha. Oh my god, this is all your fault," Ariel told Jared.

Jared said, "No, I had no idea he would find out, but somehow he knew. Somehow, he has something to do with her death. I have to get proof first or else the cops will just question him and let him go. I have never known Levy to be that type of person. I don't know what I married."

Ariel said, "You're a cheater. You broke your commitment to him, and that's why my friend is dead. Why can't you men just say no? Why is it that you all cheat and you have your woman or man whatever you have at home?

"People go crazy behind the person that they love. Some people can walk away from their cheating lives. Some will stay in and keep getting treated the same way over and over with disrespect and allowing that to continue on because they don't know any better. People kill, commit suicide, just do stupid things because of the lies, the betrayals, the heartaches, and the pain. Just stupid, stupid, stupid, stupid.

"Okay. We have to do something, because my friend doesn't deserve to be dead right now." Ariel started crying again. "I should have been there for her," she said.

Jared sat there, thinking what he could do to prove that his husband killed Sasha.

While sitting in Sasha's office, thinking, the lights went off. The sounds of guns went off. People were screaming, and Jared and Ariel jumped up. Jared peeped out the door and could see people running. Some people were lying dead on the floor, but he couldn't see who was shooting.

Ariel started screaming, crying, and panicking. Jared told Ariel to quiet down as he closed the door and started pushing the desk and chair behind the door. Ariel was on the phone, trying to call the police, but there was no dial tone or signal.

"What are we going to do?" asked Ariel.

"I don't know. People is going fucking crazy." Jared turned off the lights to throw off a distraction to the office.

Someone started banging on the door loudly. *Bang, bang, bang,* and then the banging stopped. Jared started creeping to the door, and he heard, "Honey, it's me. Open the door. I miss you. I need you." It sounded like his husband.

Jared said, "Levy, is that you?"

Levy said, "Yes, it is, and I am coming to get my man, because as I said, no one can or will ever take my man."

"Levy!" Jared called out. There was no answer. There was loud knocking on the door by Levy, who was yelling, "Open the damn door, Jared! Open the damn door, Jared!"

"No, the police is already on their way. You crazy! You killed innocent people out there, Levy. What has gotten into you?" Jared asked.

"Until death do us part," Levy said.

Jared started trying to redial the police over and over again, but still no signal, and poor, scared Ariel was just shaking and crying as she hid behind Sasha's old desk; she didn't know where to go, what to do. The office sat on the fourth floor.

For hours, there was no noise, and as Jared placed his ear to the door, he could hear the sound of tire noises. As he started backing up from the door, Levy drove a forklift straight through the office door. Jared's face barely missed the forks. Ariel started running toward the door, screaming as Levy grabbed her and held her in a choking position and said, "Bitch, you're going nowhere. You are going to tell me why you're up here, alone with my husband." Levy looked up at Jared and said, "Is this what you left our house for? Is she the one you love?"

Jared said, "No, Levy. She has nothing to do with this."

Levy stared at Jared with his big eyes, as if they were about to pop out the sockets, and he started laughing and said, "So all of a sudden, you fucking women now? So what? You not liking it one way no more? Or you unhappy with me?" Levy asked as he started crying, rubbing Ariel's hair as if she were a puppy.

Ariel said, "I have nothing to do with whatever this is."

"Shut up, child," Levy said as she threw Ariel to the floor over by Jared. "I want the both of you to take off all your clothes."

Jared said, "But, Levy, you don't have to do this."

Levy reached in his coat and pulled out a gun and said, shaking his head, "Oh yes, I do. Isn't this where it started? Isn't that the same desk, the same chair, and the same office you fuck that bitch Sasha in?" As levy stepped on the broken door where it had Sasha's name printed on it, he said, "Yep." Levy laughed. "It sure the fuck is. Now you got this pie-face bitch in here, this little thot."

Jared said, "Levy, you have it all wrong, baby."

Levy yelled, "Shut up!" as he pointed the gun at Jared. "Now take off the fucking clothes."

Ariel and Jared stripped out of their clothes and stood there naked.

Levy climbed on the forklift and said, "Now you two start making passionate love."

"What?" Jared said. Levy fired one shot and said, "You heard me, mutherfucker. Start making passionate love."

Jared and Ariel started caressing each other as Ariel was crying and wiping her tears. Levy said, "Move faster than that!" So Jared stuck his dick inside of Ariel and started stroking her and making love to Ariel.

Levy blew a whistle and said, "Stop!" As he climbed down the forklift and walked toward them, he bent down in Ariel's face and asked, "Are you handicap, bitch?"

Ariel responded, "No."

Levy slapped her and said, "Well, fuck back!"

Jared and Ariel began fucking again, but harder and with more action, as Levy watched. Police lights were flashing through the window. Levy peeped through the window and noticed a lot of police cars and could see them running inside the hospital. Levy told Jared and Ariel to lie down on top of each other and place his dick back in her and start kissing, and they did just that as Levy shot both of them to death.

Levy bent down and kissed Jared and said, "Only death could make us part, not any bitch." He took Jared's blood and rubbed it all over him as he stood up and shot himself and tossed the gun out the window. Levy just lay there, bleeding, hurt, and crying. Levy heard the cops coming in, yelling, "Police! Is anyone alive?"

Levy yelled back, "Help! help!"

Two officers had come up on him, and they yelled, "Get a paramedic up here! We have a live one!"

The paramedics rolled Levy out and announced twenty people dead. Levy was taken and treated at another hospital, away from the tragic scene, and was questioned by the police. Two weeks later, he was released into the hands of an old lady who took care of him while he healed from the devastating attack that happened at the hospital, where many people have died and where he caught his husband cheating with another woman and got caught up in a fatal shooting. The gunman was not caught. The tragic shooting made headlines for two months, and still, no killer was caught.

Levy was at home, getting nurtured by the old lady, who fed him and bathed him until he was able to come out of the shock and be able to be himself again. The police still questioned Levy for a few months and later didn't bother him again because there were still no answers and no sign of a killer. The old investigator Ernie still didn't buy Levy's story. He knew the killer was right in front of his face, but they had no evidence or witnesses that would tie Levy to the murders.

Ernie tried and tried to pin the murders on Levy, but the courts couldn't, because they had nothing but a clean gun with no prints and a lot of lives that were taken from families, friends, and loved ones. They had thought Levy had lost his state of mind because of the loss of his husband, but he was innocent until proven guilty. The case went cold.

The old lady sat at the dinner table and poured her some tea as she looked up and said, "Okay, son. You can stop it now. It's done and over with."

Levy sat still for ten minutes and looked up at his mom and started laughing.

His mother finally made parole and was released six months ago. Her favorite spot was the park where she met her monster lover and where she ran to when she just wanted to cry out, so she hung out there ever since she was released. She met some interesting folks. She even felt as if she were their angel who was trying to warn them about the bad things.

The world was quiet. There was no sound of the people in it, not even the sound of birds. It was sunny and beautiful outside.

"My son and I decided to walk the park and start all over again. This time, I am going to raise him to be the man that he needs to be. I knew my son had his dad in him—that same anger, that same violence. He even looks like his dad. I knew he would need my help, that's why I sat in prison and kept going up for parole, and I finally was granted it to get out and save my son. I owe him that from taking his father's life, but I couldn't let his father love our son in no other way, so I shot him dead, because that love that he gave our little boy was no kind of father's love. Levy and I will not love again"—Mother laughed, saying those words—"at least, I don't think."

The candle lighting was held out on the grounds where the hospital used to be until the tragic shooting happened that killed those people. Later, they tore down the building. Levy attended the candle lighting. As he lit his own candle and placed it by Jared's photo, he dropped heavy tears and whispered, "Why? Why did you do me so wrong? How come you stopped loving me?" He cried louder and louder. "How come you left me alone in this world?"

Levy noticed people staring at him, so he got up, wiped his tears, and looked at the people and then looked down at Jared's photo and said, "You do better off with your bitches anyway. Now you're with two of them." He walked off.

Levy and his mother moved out of the state, and two years later, Levy married and adopted two little kids—a boy and a girl. They lived a happy life and family. Levy had the love and loyalty and his mother's attention.

Sasha's adoptive mother, Mrs. Jessie, thought about Sasha every day. She cried to herself and even hung posters about catching Sasha's killer. One killer got away when Sasha's mother's life had ended by the hands of her grandmother, but Sasha's killer will not. Jessie started having group sessions, and a lot of men and women joined even though they knew the image that Sasha left. But many thought it could be someone in their family, or many just did not give a damn about Sasha and blamed her for what happened, and they just wanted to catch the killer who just took the lives of their loved ones that worked at the hospital.

Jessie asked, "Have you ever thought about life, life within itself? Have you ever wondered why people are the way that they are? Have you ever wondered why you haven't achieved anything in life? Have you ever wondered why you can't enjoy yourself every time you step out?

"It's the company you keep, like the mess makers, the people who have to be in the club every day of the week as if they have no life, the hoes that open their legs to every man that look like they have money by driving fancy cars/trucks or even just dress nice, the ones that have money but yet the bitch lights get shut off every month, yet the man you're fucking had money, from the enemy that awaits to try and take what you have from your man, hope to live in your house, and hope to wear your shoes. The high standards of thinking you're better than the next, the mugging of another woman because you straight dislike how she looks, how happy she is, how you just do not like her for no reason—straight hating.

"I hear women all the time, making comments—she thinks she's all that—'Look at that bitch. She is nothing but a hoe' or 'I don't like that slut' and don't even know the woman in any kind of way, just bringing hatred toward that person, give her a title because of jealousy. I hear women all the time saying, 'I don't have no worries,' yet some of you sit there in worry about other women, about how she wears her hair and makeup and how she dresses, whom she's sleeping with, or wonder what she's doing to keep him. If I am not mistaken, that's worry."

One woman raised her hand and said, "But Sasha was a hoe, and she didn't care about nobody but herself."

Mrs. Jessie just stared and said, "Look, I might not know everything, because a lot of you might ask how come I didn't stop my daughter from doing what she had done or change who she was. I raised Sasha the best that I could, loved her very much, so much. You never really know the whole story, never really know a person, period. Many people grow up and become someone different. People's mind-set change." Mrs. Jessie cried as she was speaking to the people. Mrs. Jessie and others really did not know who killed Sasha or the others. Mrs. Jessie just assumed it was a woman that went mad over a man. Everyone heard different stories.

"Women, we have to do better. Confidence is everything, and each individual should have it. And the people we see out there with low self-esteem problems, we need to lift them up and help build confidence within them. We as women need to come together instead of go against each other all the time. Hate is shown through so many women, and it is ridiculous. The sad part about it is, the woman sometimes doesn't even know that other woman and still talks about her—sad, sad, sad."

Mrs. Jessie has always wondered for a long time about life and how it repeats itself through generations. "I watch relationships, characters, marriages, people interactions with others, and lifestyles of many, not because I'm nosy, but because I have always wondered why people do the things they do, when there is more in life to keep them focused, busy, and staying positive at all times.

"Some people are blinded by the same spot of hatred that they don't see that it's not getting them anywhere but in the same situation, with no change in their lifestyle, which causes them to build bad influence and be all alone by themselves, wondering why no one wants to be around them or have them feeling as if there's no one they can turn to, not taking time to think it's the negativity that lies within them that pushes other people away. Most women think it's all about competition in their world, who wears the nicest outfit. Well, in their words, the slang talk is *cutest outfit*, better yet, 'I am the bad bitch,' as she would say, which is someone who assumes she looks better than the other woman or chick. Or should I say, 'Who can have this guy?' or 'I can sleep with her man if I wanted too'? Just stupid. What does one accomplish out of that? Answer is, nothing. My daughter died in someone's hands." Mrs. Jessie cried. "But she still didn't deserve to get her life taken no matter what she did. Her action spoke louder than words. My daughter cried for help. It was a time to help change her. All her friends didn't help, and no one did.

"Ladies, we have to help each other out. Even the little caring words could help change a person or have a person thinking they should. We women are so far separated in so many ways that if we come together, we can be very powerful. Instead women don't think like that, because we're so busy trying to run each other to the ground. If a woman does have respect for herself, a hateful woman will make it seem as if she's a tramp, a hater, jealous of whatever or whomever that targets you to do the wrong thing.

"Women are so busy trying to destroy one another, where they are not focusing on the bigger things in life, such as learning, teaching, caring for one another, and coming together. It is okay to give a positive compliment toward another woman, to tell another woman what a nice outfit she has or tell her 'I love your shoes' or 'Nice hairstyle' or 'Nice job.' Women give their own style of criticism, which is a means of destruction built to tear one another down. There are a lot of people that are designed and built around different lifestyles, that have different teaching methods, and some are just adapted to different ways—selfish, hateful, or ignorant ways. Sometimes people have the definition of *opinion* wrong."

Mrs. Jessie had the people's attention as she kept talking. "There are many ways that can destroy one another, that cause one to kill, to go crazy, to fight, or to fear, causing people to segregate, forming different groups that have their own beliefs of how one think they're better than the others or tougher than the others. If you really look into the box, it's just full of messed-up minds that haven't put it together yet. Groups don't make you, but the mind does.

"There are times when women were once friends, known as best friends, and grew up together, smiled together, had ladies' night out, and even enjoyed each other's company, but fall out and decide to tell each other's business, make up rumors about each other because of the upset, anger, and jealousy that were built up among them. Pitiful, I must say. There is nothing adult or mature about that situation, ladies. Jealousy is in every woman, and majority of women will never admit to that.

"Jealousy is what brings on the hatred among most women, because of the different looks, style, long hair, short hair, no hair, round face, long face, dress style, walking style. Ladies, there are different looks. All women don't look the same, and there is nothing you can do to change that. Beauty is within you. You ladies need to learn to accept who you are, and not accept the person that you try to be, because your face will still look the same as it did when you first looked in the mirror. Your skin tone will still be the same no matter how you dress it up, powder it up. The only thing you are able to change is the mind. The different looks of people are unique. People just need to learn how to accept it.

"Women, your business is your business. There is no need to share it with people you call your best friend, your pretend sister, coworker, neighbor, or anybody, but the one you have a problem with, that caused you to want to talk to someone. Use your mind to think. Work out your problems with the one that caused you to have the problem. No one can solve your problems but yourself. People can give you as much advice as they want, but you have to be the one that makes the decision you have to live with. Think about it. Ask yourself, have all the things, questions, secrets been kept in like you wanted it to? Or somehow it accidently got out, or the person that you told said, 'But I only told such and such and that was all. I didn't think she will say nothing.'

"Ladies, your secrets are better yet kept to yourselves. Telling other women about problems you and your man have is not okay. Not only do they take it and tell the whole world, but you will have some that use that as a target, to reach out to your man and help him ease his mind off you. They lure themselves in your place, because some women already want what you have. They are the ones that are always at your house every day as if they have no life, the ones that ring your phone more than an average person, the ones that ask where your man is, the ones that get too comfortable hugging and kissing your man on the cheek, the ones that call your man their best friend. Please, a man doesn't have a woman as a best friend. Don't fall in that trap.

"Ladies, there are so many doors that you all open because it's a blind side that you try not to see, but your enemies lie beside you, watching your every move. That's when you're supposed to notice and set the distance on far things would go. You'll know where the line is drawn.

"There are different types of women, not just the way they look, but the way they think is different too. I have friends, and they don't think like I do. Some of my friends are with different ways, but at the same time, I know how far I can go with each individual. If you have a friend that thinks it's okay to sleep with different people, know that you don't want to bring that around your man. Not saying you can't trust your partner, it just to keep her from tempting and bringing problem into your home and, better yet, to keep you from having to beat her ass, not because of the guy, but because of the disrespect. Don't let women like that get too comfortable. Don't open doors that you can't close. Women that always have something to say, always in a mess, know your limits with them too. Know that you can't go to the club with that type of woman because you're going to have an altercation and your night will be ruined.

"A woman that's always crying to you about a problem about a man every day, knowing this woman barely has long-term relationships. She tries new ones every blue moon and has problems with all of themshe cannot be the best advisor or counselor to help you with your problems, because she haven't figure out her problem yet.. That's a red flag. Distance yourself. A woman that can tell you every day that she saw your man here, there, with this person, that person, says, 'Girl, he said this to me or that to me'— red flag. Distance yourself. She has too much time on her hand, watching your man. These website that allows people to chat, if your man is Facebook friends with the same friend that you talk too on day to day bases, but you're not on that same page red flag. People post pictures of themselves, send inbox messages secretly, that they don't want their significant other to know about. The social media is a Red flag for couples, marriages and any other relationship, especially when there is no trust. That web allows you to keep in contact with each person to know what they are doing, where they are going, and also a secretly fucking connection other than picking up the phone to call each other or even set up a date, many secret affairs is created through inboxes amongst friends and random people and still these type people laugh and grin in your face while liking each statues but hooking up secretly through inbox, open up your eyes, red flag.

Mrs. Jessie kept holding meetings every chance she got, because the turnout was full each time. There were people who listened, and there were people who wanted to change but didn't know how because there was no guidance.

"Think, ladies. Don't open a door that you can't close. You don't have to dislike women. You have to distinguish the inner person, who that person really is and how is that person. Know who surround you. Put distance in between your life and others'. I have always told myself that you can become the company you keep, but if you distance yourself and know your place, you can avoid from making a fool out of yourself. Women are always talking about other women but are not paying attention to their own flaws because they are too busy in everyone else's business. Women try to always subscribe themselves to someone else's identity, but they will never be that other person. They will just keeping living that lie.

"A person can always get what they want, but it's the need that counts. You need that man to treat you like that other woman, not happening. You need that man to love you like that other woman [laughing], not happening. You need that man to put you in a nice car, not happening. You need that man to pay your bills [laughing], not happening. You need that man to be there [laughing out loud], not happening. You could never be that other woman. You can always take a woman's place but never wear her shoes, nor get the things she had or was given, nor be that woman. You will only live a lie, and the only need that you will need is a shoulder to cry on when that man you claim you wanted and got leaves you with a broken hurt, a messed-up mind, and a life of hurt, because you thought you took another woman's place, but you didn't have what he needed to be kept in his presence. You could never be another woman.

"Beautiful ladies, the drama among us can be avoided if we stop living lies, stop the jealousy, the hatred, and stop trying to be someone that we are not, setting standards so high that we forget we have to set our foot at the bottom before we get to the top.

"Ladies, another thing, we as women think we can change men. Men change themselves. If we as women act mature and respect ourselves, then the men won't attack our weakness, and they will respect us as well.

"Check yourself first. A man is going to be a man, of course, but what you give a man to play with, he will play with. If you lose yourself and allow a man to mistreat you, it sets his mind to think he can get you when he wants, however and whenever, and still have as many women as he wants in your face. Don't allow you to be disrespected. It's degrading to a woman. All I'm saying is, ladies, we are our own being, with different thoughts, different opinions, and different lives, but we are all in the same little world. If we study ourselves and correct ourselves first, then life itself will be a lot smoother.

"Most people in this world need to define *unity, respect,* and *loyalty* to learn to come together and not against one another. Ladies of the same race, learn to love yourselves. Stop worrying about the other ladies and judging them. If it's not you, why worry? Ladies—not all, but most—seem to worry and focus on other ladies when they don't even have themselves together.

"Every woman is their own individual. She can be what she wants to be, dress how she wants to dress, and wear her hair how she wants to wear it. What does she have to do with you? Or you, a woman, and you notice all the other women's flaws. What are you doing with your life? Ladies, you have too much free time in your hands in order to focus on someone else. Ladies, if you have to focus so hard on different women, then every woman is a threat to you. Every time you see a woman you have to judge, then you have a lot of insecurity issues with yourself.

"Ladies, stop trying to judge one another and try to uplift one another. All the hatred comments that some of you women say about each other are ridiculous at the end of the day. That woman is still going to be her, so stop the hatred and start uplifting each other. It is going to be okay. Ladies, it is okay to tell another woman she is beautiful. It's okay to give another woman compliments. Ladies, it is okay to accept another woman's advice. It is okay, ladies, to uplift one another.

"The competitiveness among people is ridiculous. Instead of competing with the way a person looks, dresses, talks, and walks, learn to set goals to increase your own lifestyles to make your life a better one, where you do not have time to even worry about the next, but can lean toward helping those that need a lift.

"When marriages, relationships, friendships, leaderships start falling apart, it's not because it was not meant to be or this other lady or man cheated or because we fuss and argue too much, but because of the lack of respect, strong bonds, loyalty, trust, unity, and the ability to say 'No, this is not what I signed up for. This is not right. This is going to start an argument. This is not the words I have given to people, myself, my spouse, or my friend.' Know the problems that come your way. Know how to handle the situation, and correct it to avoid unnecessary stress or losing someone close to you over nothing.

"When you have someone good in your life, learn to hold on to them, because someone else will be quick to snatch them up with no problem, and then you will see how good you had it with the one you let go. Personal business is personal business. Never tell any or every one your problems within your relationships, because somehow your business will end up around the world . People gossip spreading there bestfriends business, talking about one friend with another, sleeping with each other partner and smiling about it, and even make up untrue rumors. Those type of people have a lot of time on their hands, especially the ones with nothing to do with their life, where so many problems are going on in their relationships that they're so busy with other folks, where they can't correct their problems. Misery loves company. It's okay to have friends, best friends, homeboys or home girls, but it's not okay to share any important personal matters with them, because these homeboys, home girls, best friends, friends will eventually fall out. Some move away, and some get upset because they disagree on something, or they start getting jealous, where they spread all your business. Some friends even think it is okay to sleep with your significant other or your ex.

"Ladies, have more respect for yourselves. No, it's not okay to do any of that. Or you weren't a friend from the start. Some of your enemies, and long down the line enemies, sit right there next to you. Some even wait in line just for you to make them your close home girl. Just keep an eye for the sneaky look or the clingy-type girl or the ones who never spoke to you or the ones who stare you up and down with that weird stank look as if she doesn't like you or the ones who are always having negative things to say instead of positive things.

"Another thing, ladies of all color, stop letting women get to comfortable with your man. That to me is a problem waiting to happen. Stop letting women get too comfortable where they are at your house twenty-four seven, where sometimes they don't know how to go home. Meet somewhere else sometimes, like in a bar, a restaurant, a Wings to Go place, somewhere else besides your home, because you have your women, thirsty women, who are waiting for you to fall short. There are negative women always trying to bring you down. Their lives haven't gone anywhere. You have your women that can't keep a man but always have advice, telling you what you should and shouldn't do.

"Ladies, another thing where women seem to mess up at. Hear this out now! Ladies, if you and your man stay together, there should be no other woman or man getting comfortable in your house. When your man comes home from work, nobody should be there but you and your man. Ladies, don't open a door you can't close. Ladies, stop trying to go after a man that is already taken, because if you can pull him from that woman, another woman can steal him from you, and that's when all your little insecurities come in the relationship, because you know just how you got him. Any man can be taken if they let themselves be taken. Any many can get a hoe, but a man is not going to keep a hoe and not even think twice about her. Any man can get a woman. Whether he lets her go or keep her, he is going to always think of her and wish he would have held on to her.

"They say diamonds are a woman's best friend, because women are genuine, soft, nice, and emotional and can be loyal to her man. They say dogs are men's best friend, because men like dogs. No! No! No! Ladies, dogs are men's best friend because they have so many similarities. If you let a man run around loose, he is going to be out of control. If a man runs around, sleeping with multiple women, he's a stray [stray dog], hot and ready with whomever and whenever. If a man is hissing at you, he is barking like a dog. Ladies, your name isn't a hissing song. Men need to approach you in a good-manner tone, such as 'Excuse me, miss' or 'Excuse me, ma'am.'

"If a man gets caught, he starts whining like a mutt, trying to cover his tracks with all those excuses. Ladies, if you don't train your man and learn to put your foot down and don't take any kind of disrespect and don't lay some rules and regulations down, you will have a man that's a dog and will dog you out in so many ways. But if you handle your business and get some understanding, you will have for yourself a man that comes home at a decent time and only love one woman, and that is you. Ladies, stop thinking it's okay for your man to be out there cheating. Because he comes home to you at night, that doesn't mean you have him, that doesn't mean he is your man. Lessons are to be learned, and what one learns is to be taught.

"In life there are many temptations that people overloads their minds with, the thoughts and the visions that one assumes that at that particular moment, whatever the temptation was, it could fix or change whatever they're trying to get. They still made that choice. They still let the mind take control, and at the end of the day, afternoon, or morning, that person is still accountable for his or her actions, because the body only does what the mind tells it to do.

"If a person wants to say no, best believe it could be said. There is no excuse for one's action, because for one, if a person knew that his or her mind would start to wander, he or she could have taken themselves out of that position by thinking of something else, by not looking at that person or whatever drawing the attention to his or herself. People make their own decisions. One can't blame others for one's own action.

"Every woman wants to feel special. Every woman is special, and an individual should not have to put up with so little or so much verbal abuse, domestic abuse, drug abuse, and substance abuse. Every person is special. Most of us just need to surround ourselves with positive people, and whatever is stressing one's self, you need to wing yourself out of that situation and get yourself together. Make changes in your life, and find happiness. Life is too short. Look in the mirror. That is God's creation. Anything God created is special. No need to hear it from someone else or go through abuse to feel some type of way. In life, a person never knows what one goes through. In life, you never know what a person is going through. All the judging folks, the bullying, the assaults, the deaths, and the suicides that happen throughout this world happen for numerous of reason: lack of love, respect, or parenting, as well as embarrassment, abuse, trash talk, rumors, poverty, and the judging of others.

"This world is not a screwed-up place. This world is just a place. This world has a lot of things in it that is manmade to give people something to look at, to grow, to learn, and to help develop more of this created world. This world is just a world we people live in. We build homes, create businesses, plant trees, build highways, build roads to travel on, have kids, get jobs, and make money. People build lives, people build and develop things, and we as people make our life the way that it is. You can choose to be a better person, a helper, creator, listener, lover, friend, teacher, cop, process operator, homeowner, mother, father, or whoever you choose to be. People, whatever choice or decision you make in life, you make it on your own, by your own self. It's not 'He or she made me do it,' 'He or she said it,' or 'I thought it was this.' No. When your mind starts thinking and you are unsure about things, seek to define the truth, the right answer, or the right solution, because if you make a decision, it's you alone that made that choice, no matter how many people gave you advice. At the end of the day, it's whether or not you made the right choice.

"The news/media, newspaper, magazines, Facebook, Instagram, Twitter—people create those sites, and we people create profiles. We as people give them what we choose to give them. If you share your business, troubles, argument, personal matters, killings, stealing, drugs, or any other business of yours, you choose to do so. You choose to put that out there. Stop giving people something to talk about. Stop giving people something that they could tear you down with. Stop doing things like stealing, and you could just get a job and buy it. Stop making people's problems your problems. Stop killing people because of anger, jealousy, rage, guilt, lack of love, lack of responsibility—that is not your call.

"Ladies, stop selling yourself short. Stop stripping, prostituting, and using excuses like 'Well, it pays my bills,' 'I have to make a living,' or 'I have to take care of my kids.' The same amount of hours you put in at a strip club, you can put in at a real job, and saying things like 'I make more money at a strip club than a regular job.' Well, ladies, a regular job gets you benefits, a check, and respect. A strip job gets you money, half-naked outfits, bad reputation, name-calling, and a hard time finding a man. One-nighters don't count. Men that pay you for your service don't count. That's how come the club owner gave you that title, that pole, and those naked clothes to do as you are told. You signed up for that job. Nobody did it for you.

"Women come up missing every day. Women are raped every day, and children are molested every day and found dead, buried and in trash bags, because of lack of parent skills, attention, and the role models that people choose to be. Someone is always watching you.

"Mothers, when you have children, love them, give them your full attention, manage your life, accept a job that fits your life time, so within that day or in the middle of the week, you at least can be in that child's life. Money is good, but working long hours and not making time for your family can hurt you, especially that child. Money can buy so many things in this world, but it can't buy time, a mother's attention, a mother's love, or the small things to notice when it comes to a child. Ladies, stop allowing yourself to go through things where you end up taking it out on your children, and stop having yourself dressed up but your child looking raggedy and abandoned. Ladies, stop selling your food stamps when you have seven kids to feed. Stop abusing your kids.

"People's minds are like computers. They start recognizing things, programming, storing, receiving, deleting, accepting, organizing, and reprogramming it and catching viruses. That's how people become delusional, dysfunctional, psychopaths, killers, child molesters, jealous, evil, etc., because of the things they went through in life, the things they had no control of in life while they were kids. And of course one has his or her own mind, but it starts from home. It starts from parenting. That's how come it is very important to be the parent, to be in your child's life. If you can't take care of your child, at least care about that child and give the child up for adoption. At least you made the right choice. Ladies, we have to do better. Ladies, you have to have respect for yourselves. You have to stop accepting the disrespect from men and each other.

"If you respect yourself and have respect for others, you will be recognized in a positive way. Not even the harsh words can harm you. Men are going to be men. They can only be what you allow them to be, what you accept, and what you put up with and carry on with. If a man can get away with things, he will do so. If you sell yourself short to him, he is going to spend every bit of it and keep shorting you. Have respect, get respect, get order, and accept no other.

"Ladies, have stamina about yourself when it comes to putting up with so many situations that do not benefit a purpose in your life. Don't settle for less. Settle for the best. Want more in life. It takes time for doors to open, but when it does, you will know it. All the hard work, the stressing, and the strong person that you become, believe and you will get where you need to be in life. Everything you do in life has a path you have to take before you reach your destination. It depends on how far you want to go, how bad you want it, and how important it is for you to continue that path to reach your point. Just believe, and it will be in your favor.

"Respect is what every person in this world should want, but if you don't have it for yourself or even notice the things you do that you think is respectful, it only sends out negative thoughts to folks, such as the clothes you might wear, the company that you keep, the way you do things, and especially the attitude. A woman can wear an attitude that is so ugly that it makes everything about her ugly.

"Ladies that have children, some not all, you all know who you are. Stop using them as bait. Stop abusing, giving up, starving, killing, abandoning, leaving a hurt little heart that cries every night, wishing they could have another parent. These children need a mother. The children need you, your full attention, the attention that nobody could give them but you, the mother that birthed him or her, that carried him or her in her womb for months. Many hearts go out to children, and many shed tears and cry in silence because of the children's situations, which could be avoided if parents would be parents, if mothers would protect and give their full attention toward their children to know when the good or bad is heading that way. You are that child's protector. Ladies, protect your children. Stop trying to get attention, and give it to the one or ones who need it, your child your children. Ladies, we need to open up our minds and start thinking more about the important things in life, what is important and what is not.

"Videos that are recorded and placed on websites of females fighting, waves getting pulled out, bras getting ripped off. Oh my, so embarrassing. There is no fame, no spotlight, no checks that come with your name on it, and no point in any of that nonsense, but laughter, gossip, jail, and/or a bad police record that could ruin your life. Ladies, that is not cute. Get your together. Ladies, no matter what you do, no matter how long you wait, some things will never change. There is always opportunity to become a better person, so wipe your slate clean and start all over.

"Love yourself, respect yourself, don't neglect yourself, don't stress yourself, don't downgrade yourself, just adjust yourself, and don't let the world gossip destroy yourself.

"People are beautiful no matter what color, size, height, or hair. Your personality, your attitude can either break you or make you, but you have to accept the fact you are who you are. You can change who you are and act as who you want to be, but you are still you.

"Ladies, when you try so hard, you fall so easy, because the only person you fool is yourself. Foolery doesn't last forever, because the ears, the whispers, and the gossip you cause while trying so hard made the backstabbers want to test the lifestyle you're living. People become hungry because you brag so much about this, he does this and that, he bought this, 'Oh, I got this.' They become more hungry and target the things or the people you brag about, that plays a part in your life, that's causing you to be happy, even if it causes friendships to end, relationships to fail, or marriages to be corrupt. Ladies, your business is your business. You don't need to tell the whole world about it. Ladies, the only person you need to impress is yourself, and the rest will fall in place. Your secret is a secret that you should keep, because after you share it with one person, you just shared it with everybody else. Because once that person gets mad, all your baggage is spread out like butter. No one can solve your problems but yourself. You can take all the advice you want, but change starts within yourself. There's nothing wrong with a little help, but you have to keep personal business to yourself and solve that problem with the person who caused it to be so personal and then a problem. That's the only way you can solve that problem.

"What you and your man go through, keep it to yourself. Stop welcoming everyone into your life, people that do not belong in it. People gossip begins when people make up their own hatred, beliefs, lies, betrayals, jealousy, and the mouth that should have been shut without letting out her business. People run and twist words all the time.

"Ladies, it's okay to have friends, associates, or whatever you want to call the person you communicate with, but know the distance you can go with them. Everyone has a distance. With women, it's okay to have ladies' night, but have it at a club, bar, or restaurant or book a room. Keep them out your house, your business. Even if you do invite your home girl, girl friend, or whomever, have a time limit when they come in, when they clear out, because sometimes they get too comfortable. Be alert of your surroundings when you're around other women, and watch their reactions—the fake laughs, fake smiles, and clinginess. Sometimes you can tell who you are dealing with.

"Some women will say she's just jealous or insecure, has no trust. Believe it's not that. Whoever fixed their mouth to even say that, their priorities are mixed up. It's called not being dumb or blindsided by the she-devil that awaits to ruin your life or drag you in the mud and target everything you have. Some women can be so cruel, sneaky, evil, miserable, and just plain sad.

"Men and women, temptations play a part in everyone's lives, but men are a lot weaker than women. Women are more emotional, truthful, and they love hard when it comes to the love of their life and try not to do wrong. But men, temptation could get the best of them because they're so weak. Men need training on how to control their mind and body, because once their mind starts wandering, it's all over. Men and women need not put themselves in a situation in which he or she will regret or have to explain later or lose everything that was worth having to someone that was nothing but a screwup. Loyalty is important. Don't put yourself in a situation where loyalty could slip. Learn how to decline trouble that may come your way.

"Avoid and stop self-destruction. Stop punishing yourself because of personal failures. Stop the hatred. If you want attention, respect yourself, and stop attention seeking, because you will attract the wrong kind. Self-destruction is not the right way to cope. Don't be ashamed to change, ladies. Change can be a good thing, even if you start losing friends, associates, or anyone close to you, and most of the time, it's good to lose folks because they're not serving a purpose in your life, or it could be the other way around—you're not serving a purpose in their life. Changing your surroundings and the company you keep can help you a lot in keeping you out of the same situation you have been in over and over again, keeping you in nothing but mess and also keeping your stress levels up. Now if your friends want to see things differently in your life and care to support you, it is okay for that to take place, but if they're there to bring you down, release them from your life. What purpose do they serve?

"Most people hold others down instead of build them up. Knowing or seeing the situation that the other person is going through, but instead of building them up, they're feeding that person with negativity and then running to spread all that person's business to the world. Huh, some friend that is.

"A wake-up call is good for some people, but a wake-up call can bring more pain than what a person asks for. A wake-up call can be anything—death, broken heart, your own life, lost of marriage, lost job, or a bad reputation that can destroy you forever. So really, do you actually want a wake-up call, or do you want to find your inner strength and build yourself, respect yourself, and be confident with yourself, and not let yourself fall so low where you don't have to have that wake-up call because you got yourself together? You pick yourself up and is on time that you didn't need anything to wake you up.

"The more you engage with people that put you down, argue with you, fight, talk behind your back, continue doing hateful things, always talking about others, cheat, and abuse you, the more you string yourself to be in the situation you're in, because you can't let go. Well, let go. You know when things are not right. You know bullying someone is not right. You know telling of your friends' business is not right. You know sleeping with your friend or a married man is not right, or smoking weed or doing drugs other than for looking for a job is not right. You know fighting or jumping someone is not right. You know scratching cars, breaking windows, killing, stealing, abusing mentally, physically, and emotionally are not right. You know not taking care of your kids is not right. You know child neglect and child abuse are not right.

"People, your brain thinks before it reacts. Only you sometimes avoid what you're thinking because you're angry or trying to please others, and you always say after you did something wrong, 'Oh, I was not thinking.' Yes, you were. You had to think and plan exactly what you were going to do and how you were going to do it before you even did it, so you were thinking, and your brain was working just fine. Just like when a man cheats on his wife or girlfriend, the first thing he cries when his woman finds out is, 'Baby, I am sorry. I wasn't thinking. It was a mistake' or 'It was like this. She came on to me. Baby, she means nothing. It was just sex, nothing more, she's nothing.' Okay, he wasn't thinking, but he remembered how it was and what it meant. People say things instead of being truthful and keeping their words and not doing wrong in the first place.

"It's a hurtful feeling in this world when it comes to some women who have their priorities mixed up. Ladies, when you have kids, those kids are your seeds. Those babies grow, and they need you more than anything and anyone. Hearing a baby cry for help is the worst sound ever. Kids come before anything. It is sad that in this world, there are women who sell the help that is given to them to benefit them, their household, until they are able to get back on their feet to become more self-sufficient. The hurt comes when you see starving kids around this world when the mother gets food stamps to purchase the food for their household to feed their kids yet sell all their stamps for a little bit of cash that's a lower amount, but they have four, five, or six kids to feed. Forget the hair, the makeup. Get your life together. Those kids need you more than anything. If your belly is full, your kid's belly needs to be full. If your hair is combed, your kid's hair needs to be combed. Don't abuse the kids. Love, cherish, and keep the kids growing.

"Single ladies, it's okay to be single and not married or belong to a man, but it is not okay to open your legs up to any, any number of guys, or everybody. Enjoying life is not that. That is your reputation getting destroyed and you don't even know it. You don't even see it coming because you are too blind to see it. You're too busy trying to get attention. You're too busy being blinded by society and the celebrity world until you got it all twisted, and no, you don't have to be a celebrity, but why are you out there doing big things like drinking, smoking, sleeping with Tom, Dick, and Harry, and partying? You better be able to pick your face up and clean yourself up. And no, that is not being on top. That's being on the bottom, because at the end of the day, a man wants a woman that respects herself. It is okay to have fun and enjoy your life, but make sure it's something you won't regret, and make sure something good comes out of it in the long run, like success and becoming successful in what you're doing. Respect yourself.

"Married women, stop blaming yourself when your husband messes up. Stop listening to the mistress or the other woman saying, 'Well, you should have handled your business, or he wouldn't be over here' or 'I am better than you' or 'Well, he wanted this,' because at the end of the day, she was the temptation that whispers among men. There are wrongful people that stir the pot, knowing exactly what they do when they do it. You have the devils and the angels, and no, the man is not right for cheating at any point, but trust and believe that no matter what happens with that other woman, it's only one woman he thinks of and how he's going to explain himself too, and that's the woman he loves. Problems start at home, because two people don't communicate as much as they need to. There are boundaries that need to be established. Give each other space, allowing one to clear his or her mind and be able to miss you a little, but not too much or else it would be an opportunity for someone to ease their way in that spot or even slip up. .

"If a man cheats once, do forgive him and work out the problem and find out what went wrong. If a man continues to cheat over and over again, causing you to hurt over and over again, hurt no more and let him go. Don't do any more harm to your heart, your body, your soul, or your mind. You can't save something that doesn't want to be saved, because it takes the two who were joined by hand in marriage, not one. Ladies, stop saying another woman was the cause of the marriage coming to an end, because it wasn't her that put the ring on your finger, and you have to remember he stepped out his marriage. He should have just said no, even though she knew he was married or even knew who you were.

"Those wrongful people are among us. We have people that are ready to destroy and tear people down, and if anybody let those devilish people get them off track, because they're not strong enough to run a straight line, then they too need to pump up some iron and build up some muscle to hold a strong backbone to protect his or her relationship and defeat the devils and catch whatever is thrown at him or her.

"Life too short to end up in avoidable situations. Don't drive yourself to a place you did not ask to be. Don't tell the whole world your problems, because they can't solve your problems. They can only give advice or spread your business, but only you can solve your problems. Seek belief in yourself. Be confident and strong. You do have a lot of good people out in this world. It's hard to fall down when you have so many people to hold you up, but the right people.

"Ladies, we need to stop with the hatred, belittling each other, and learn to keep the faith and stop trying to please the wrong people by downgrading your own people. In this society, don't label yourself the wrong way. No, you can't get an applause for being rude and disrespecting your own kind. It only makes you look even more stupid, and others use you as their gossip dummies. How is someone going to respect and trust a person that's always running their mouth about other people? People listen all the time what someone has to say, because who doesn't want to hear the gossip? But trust and believe that while you are gossiping, the people you're gossiping with are gossiping about you too. No one will trust a person that gossips all the time. Some of the gossip might be true, and some might be false, but if it is not your business, why stick your nose in it, especially when you were not invited in personally?

"If someone trusts you enough to tell you their business, why betray that trust and tell the whole world that person's business? Messing up, dishonesty, betrayal, and gossip will leave you alone, used, or worse yet, miserable, because you will always fall flat on your face, because everybody knows not to tell Mrs. Messy or trust Mrs. Messy. And you wonder why things are going wrong in your life. That's because you're so busy minding everyone else's business that you did not focus enough to catch up with your own because you left it so far behind while you were all up in somebody else's.

"Ladies, come together. Ladies, lean on each other instead of always being against each other. Ladies, we are delicate flowers. We bloom so beautifully, but some turn so ugly by their ugly ways. If ladies work together to lean on each other, this world would be filled with all different sorts of beautiful, delicate flowers. We might look different, walk different, are shaped different, with different style, laughter, and even have a different heart, but, ladies, when you all come together, your presence will be stronger than anything that comes your way. Learn to love, respect, and be stronger. You can rule the world, ladies, with a strong deliverance toward each other, by uplifting and loving one another.

"Do you all know how it is right now for each and every young or older lady? No, you all do not, because each and every one of you is your own individual. That's how come they say do not judge a book by its cover. You never know what an individual is going through. That's how come it is good to communicate with one another, get to know one another, and leave the hatred, violence, jealousy, disrespect, and destruction out of your life. It's okay to start all over. It is a needed time to look deep down and find yourself. Some people made a lot of mistakes in their life. Okay, start over. Stop walking down the same road and patterns. Start over and learn different ways. If you start and fail, just get up and start all over. It will just make you stronger. Be totally yourself.

"Every woman is beautiful, but it's up to you to accept it instead of pretending to be someone else. If you label yourself as something or someone and you act as such, you will be known of what you act, and the world will read and accept what you give. People, you can't help others if you can't help yourself. It's okay to please others, helping others make the right choices, but don't forget about yourself. Stop doubting yourself, because it's the reason behind every doubt that runs across your mind. Find the cause of that doubt and challenge it. Prove it wrong and settle the problem.

"Ladies that went through a rough childhood growing up, what you experienced in life was something you had to deal with. The tears that dropped and the silent cries that were not heard and the whispers for help that no one paid attention to were a heartache to you. These situations start at home, and it's up to the parents to notice the troubles that the child is in, but there are some weak practices in parenting that some of you get comfortable in your own little mind that you forget about the responsibility that you have. You are your child's protector. Stay in your child's life. Know everything about your child, what he or she is going through. Know why he or she is not smiling that day or why he or she is sad, why he or she stays in his or her room all day, and ask questions twenty-four seven. Mothers that have a kid or kids, you should have him or her feeling one way about themselves and that is special and them knowing that they are, , and it's the parents' job to keep their kids uplifted and filled their minds up with good, respectful, and happy memories, child hood is everything, that is where habits are pick up, kids are learning a lot during that time and what a kid see he or she want forget, so parents catch the signs of a trouble, disturb, hurt, low self-esteem child before its too late, hear your child's cry and be the one to catch the first tear.

"What you went through as a child, don't let that be the reason you choose to doubt yourself. Don't let that be a reason your kids are raising themselves. Don't let it be a reason you shortchange yourself. Don't let that be an excuse for the bad choices you make in life. Don't let it make you less of a woman. Don't let it make you say to people, 'You don't know what I've been through.' Let it make you become a stronger person and not let it repeat itself through your older life, which you can change. Don't let your childhood memories destroy your life. Grow, learn, and teach it to others. Teach that even though these horrible things happen to you, that you have become stronger and that you won't let your children suffer or repeat what you'd been through. Because there are people crying for help every day, but we can't hear those silent cries, but we as people, if we stop the hatred among one another and start being focused on what is important in our lives and come together as a team, as other puzzle pieces, we can help out in probably making the human life a little better. No one can guarantee that the whole world would change and be fair, because it would just be a lie, because there will always be some faulty people that are looking to destroy others in some kind of way.

"Ladies, your body is not a tool. Treat your body like a temple.. The average woman needs to let go of past relationships. Don't bring it to the next relationship. Leave the baggage with him or drop it in the trash on the way out. Either way, let it go. Because when you're at home and you have trash, what do you do with it? You get rid of it, and you don't think twice about it. When it's a bad relationship, you have to leave it and stop hauling it around. It's going to become a burden. Ladies, we cry, we hurt, and when we hurt, no one can tell us different, because some always say, 'You all don't know what I have been through.'

"Ladies, if a relationship is abusive, full of lies, has a lot of cheating, full of deception and hurt, and brings pain to the heart, you need not prolong the relationship. Let go, because you will only set yourself up for failure. People can't change a person. A person has to change themselves. Ladies, learn to keep your relationship juicy. Ladies, stop wanting what you don't give. You want preferential treatment, but you're not giving it. You want a man that can cook for you, but you can't cook. You want a back rub, but you don't do back rubbing. You want head, but you don't want to give head. You like gifts, but you don't like giving. For a truthful, honest, and trustful relationship, you have to understand that fair exchange is not robbery, but truly you can't keep getting and not giving without the other person feeling as if they were being robbed.

"One of the main things women need to stop doing with one another is telling their personal business. Your relationship is personal, and that is the way it is being kept. The problem is that women talk with others about their personal problem in their relationship, while the other half of the relationship has no idea that something is wrong. No one can solve your problem but the one that you have or started the problem with. Surely, if that's what's happening, guess what? You are not in a relationship, because you don't talk about it. You straighten that out at home, and mentally you are sharing information like you do when you are in an affair, not a relationship. Ladies, some of you are in a fantasy of what a relationship really is. If this is what is happening in your life, obviously you do not know the difference between the two, an affair and a relationship. Life starts with reality, and if you're not real, well, your life is going to be fantasy. We as people, in order to be in a relationship with other people, first have to define the terms that we use with one another and the words for us to have a real relationship.

"Ladies, know the difference between dating, relationship, a booty call, and an affair. *Dating* is simply two people trying to commune with each other to see if they are compatible. A *relationship* is when two people decide to take it to the next step, to not share personal feelings and love with any other person. A *booty call* is when a person that has restrained themselves as long as they could has to have an orgasm, so they go in search for a quick sex, a partner to have sex with—no love, no dating, no relationship, just straight orgasm, and that's all its going to be. And an *affair* is two people cheating on someone else.

"Most people can't change because most think they are perfect, so they say they can't find any problems with themselves. If you can't find any problem with yourself, then you will know what needs to change, because you are good. Change is voluntarily. In order to change and be better in life, you have to first realize that you need to change, and no one can change you but yourself.

"There are times when some ladies say, 'I am his ride or die chick.' Please, ladies, if creating for yourself a jail profile, getting locked up, having a jack-up background, and/or making a bad name for yourself is considered a ride or die chick, then I would suggest you start considering something else, like an education, a career, or a clean background, because at the end, whether you ride or die with the dude, the result is that you will be either locked up, messed up, or left alone, because he will end up in jail or dead or you will. He is not going to wait on you, like you wait on him. Trust and believe that it is totally different when a woman gets locked up, because a man is not going to wait. He's going to sleep with the next woman he has in mind, but when a man gets locked up, you, his boo or wife, instead of ride or die chick—because he knows you're going to put some money on his books, a pen pal, a picture buddy, and his working buddy—work for him hard while he's locked up. People make mistakes in life and get jail time, but know when you're getting played. You can act tough and bad or fight all the time if you want to, but girls, that's what you are, girls, because women don't act like that. A woman respects herself, not degrade herself.

"Ladies that allow men to play house but don't contribute to any bills, you have to do better than that, especially for you ladies that have a child or children. Clubs? There is nothing wrong with clubs, but if you are a mom and you're in the club every weekend, I can't see how this child is getting your attention. Even though grandparents, aunts, or uncles watch them, it's nothing like a mother's love. And ladies that don't worry about their child or children because they're well taken care of, lady, you can buy all the things a kid wants or needs, but it's nothing compared to missing your child grow up and being in your child's life, because your child is going to remember every bit of what you spoiled him or her with, but they're also going to recall the time you were never there. Don't cut short what is important, for the streets, that will always be there, when you're here and when you're gone.

"Ladies, follow your mind. You know when something is wrong, and you know when something is right. Your intuition is always right, whether you can prove it or not, because you have to think, ladies. All the time, your woman intuition notified you. It was right whether you proved it to be right in a day, week, a month, and/or years—it was right.

"Another thing, ladies, when you all talk to your best friend, associate, sister, or mother about how to satisfy your man or a man in bed, your friends can give you all the tips in the world, but another woman cannot answer those questions better than the man you're having sex with, because only he can tell you what you can do to satisfy him. What works for one woman may not work for another woman, because every woman operates differently. You ladies run to all the wrong people, asking those questions about what you should do in bed with your man, or guy friend, whatever title you want to give him, and in reality, a man can only answer that question about things you can do in bed to satisfy him.

"People spend more time telling their problems instead of solving their problems. You people can set around and tell the whole your problems, but it's only one person that can solve the problem. It's the one you have it with.

"Gossipers always have a story about someone or anyone. If you have one friend that tells you about another friend, nine out of ten, that friend is talking about you too. If you have friends that are always in some mess, that means you're going to always be looked at that way, also messy, because of the company you keep. Ladies can have juicy conversations, but let it not be personal problems that other people have nothing to do with. When friends get mad, especially the friend you trusted, they end up telling all your business to the next target that they pick up as a friend. Misery loves company, but a grown woman can handle her own problems within herself without telling it to others. Of course, we all have to have someone to talk to, but talk to them with a limit. You can have a shoulder to cry on, but cry on the shoulder that hurt you so that they can see and feel your pain or at least they can know something isn't right. Whether that person stays or goes, they will remember the hurt and the cries of the woman that lay on his or her shoulder."

Mrs. Jessie spoke to young ladies and even gentlemen that attended Jessie's meeting and group sessions. Mrs. Jessie changed a lot of young ladies' lives. Mrs. Jessie spoke a lot about change and positivity. One day, she received a tip about who killed Sasha. The detective from the case told her that it was a man who was married to another guy and that he heard that Sasha had slept with his husband, so he killed her. Mrs. Jessie's heart fell. She dropped to her knees. All the hard work of speaking out to ladies and some gentlemen about positive changes and the truth about life went out the door. Meetings were not being held anymore. Mrs. Jessie didn't even pick up phone calls. Mrs. Jessie's coworkers came by to check on her. She just let them knock.

Mrs. Jessie decided to look up Levy and everything that she could find on him. She found his destination and saw where he relocated out of town. Mrs. Jessie started laughing out loud as she said, "I got you now, you murderer." Mrs. Jessie started packing up her small bag; she decided to take a trip across town. She checked herself in at a hotel two miles near Levy's home. Mrs. Jessie drove past Levy's house every chance she got so that she can get a closer look at him, to see how he looked, what he liked, and how he dressed, just looking to see what type of lifestyle he liked and what type of men he liked also.

Mrs. Jessie noticed Levy telling the kids, "Let's go, get into the car," and he drove off. She decided to follow him and watch as Levy pulled up to a park. Mrs. Jessie decided to get out and act as if she were just walking around the park so that she can get a better view of Levy. Well, at least she expected viewing was all she would be doing, but Levy ended up speaking to her. He was laughing at the kids and how they were playing together, and then he just started a conversation, asking if she had any kids. Mrs. Jessie looked up and said to him, "I once did."

Levy looked at Mrs. Jessie and asked, "If you don't mind me asking, what happened?"

Jessie said, "Oh, she just happened to be picked to be an angel in heaven."

Levy looked and smiled and said, "At least she is in a better place," and rubbed Mrs. Jessie on her back.

Levy and Mrs. Jessie sat at the park for at least two hours, talking. He even told her about his love life, his marriage, his loving mother, and how his life was the happiest life ever and that he couldn't ask for anything more.

Mrs. Jessie looked at Levy as he smiled from ear to ear, and he stated those words so proudly as if he had no hurt or no kind of sorrow, as if a tragedy never happened, as if he never even thought about the lives he had taken, as if those lives didn't even matter. Mrs. Jessie got up and said she had to go and that it was nice talking to him, and she left before a tear could even roll from her watery eyes.

Mrs. Jessie returned back to her hotel room. She took a long shower, crying as she stood, letting the water wash away her tears into the drains near her feet. Mrs. Jessie later on that night flicked through her phone, looking at Sasha's pictures, hearing the sounds of Sasha's laughter in her head. Mrs. Jessie laughed and cried heavily, thinking of her daughter, that she cried herself to sleep.

The next morning Mrs. Jessie went shopping in the men's department store. She bought a couple of suits, jeans, T-shirts, socks, boxers, sneakers, some square-toe dress shoes, and some other men items. Mrs. Jessie drove past Levy's home but did not see his vehicle, so she left and returned back to the hotel. Mrs. Jessie rested in the hotel room the rest of the day. She ironed and starched clothes, and later she shaved her head into a clean cut, low fade, like a guy. She took a shower to wash the falling cut pieces of hair off her. Mrs. Jessie even washed with men's body wash. She dried herself off and put on men's boxer brief and dabbed herself with men cologne. She duct-taped her boobs tightly to her body so that they would not stick out as much. Mrs. Jessie dressed up in men's starched jeans and button-down shirt, and she, who was now dressed as a he, left out the door. Mrs. Jessie wasn't herself anymore. She had become a different person, a person she called David.

Mrs. Jessie drove past Levy's home again, but only this time, she spotted him getting out of the car with grocery bags.

"Excuse me, sir," she yelled out in a deep manly voice. "Is there any way you can tell me where an elegant restaurant is located?" Mrs. Jessie asked.

"Sure," Levy said. "It's actually a little ways from here, but I can give you directions." As Levy started telling her the direction, he could see the confused expression on her face. "Are you from here?" Levy asked.

"No, I am actually from out of town. By the way, my name is David. I am on a small business trip."

Levy shook David's hand. "Nice to meet you." Levy said to him, "If you can wait while I put the groceries up, I don't mind showing you where the restaurant is."

"Oh, that would be great," David said.

Levy walked away to put the groceries in the house, and he returned back outside and told David, "Okay, I will pull off first, and you just follow me."

David said, "Okay."

When they arrived at the restaurant, David stepped out the car and walked up to Levy's car and said, "Thank you so much. I would have been lost."

"No problem," Levy said as he stared at David from head to toe. David looked so damn good to him.

David asked Levy if he was okay, and Levy said, "Yes, I am okay. Well, here is the place. Have a good night."

Before Levy could pull off, David asked if he would like to join him for dinner, and Levy quickly replied and said yes.

David opened Levy's car door for him, trying to be a gentlemen, and he even opened the restaurant door for Levy. Levy didn't know what to think. He was just surprised by the handsome guy whom he barely even knew. David and Levy laughed and talked all night, and they even shared a frozen daiquiri together.

It was getting late, so David said he had to get back to the hotel so that he can get some rest for the meeting tomorrow. David walked Levy to his car and made sure he had driven off first, just to be on the safe side, making sure she won't be followed back to the hotel room.

Levy returned back home, where he sat in his car, just thinking how great of a night it was. Levy's husband came outside and asked why he was outside, just sitting in the car, and why the groceries were just left out and not put up. Levy told his husband that he got called to go into work for an emergency.

David returned back to the hotel room, washed up, and thought of the next plan. David knew she had Levy right where she wanted him, his lusting eyes showed how much of an easy target he was, and by the end of the night, his action showed how desperate he was. "He will pay for my daughter's death. I won't rest until he does," Mrs. Jessie said.

At about 11:30 p.m., Mrs. Jessie's phone rang. It was Levy. David picked up the phone, and Levy asked him if he would like to hang out a little bit more because he liked his company.

David replied, "Yes, I would love that."

David and Levy made plans to have a picnic at the Lakeside Park for tomorrow. After David hung up the phone, she decided to get up and put a wardrobe together for the picnic and prepare a picnic basket. Mrs. Jessie didn't know if she should poison the picnic food or just bring a big butcher knife and stab his ass to death, but she also thought that would be too easy.

The next morning, Mrs. Jessie clean shaved and taped her boobs tightly to her body so that they would not stick out, and she hoped that she could pull off being a man again without being noticed. Mrs. Jessie got dressed. She put on some jogger pants and a nice green shirt and some nice sneakers, and she grabbed the picnic basket and headed out the door. "I can't explain how nervous I am," Jessie said out loud to herself while driving to meet up with

Levy. "I am not sure if my nerves are bad because I want to kill this man so bad or because my cover will probably be noticed."

When Mrs. Jessie arrived at the Lakeside Park, she put her David mode on and stepped out the car. Levy had already had the picnic blanket laid out by the lake, with strawberries and wine.

"Hi, David," Levy said as he leaned over and gave him a kiss on his cheek.

"Hi," David said back as they sat and prepared themselves for their loving evening.

They sat, talked, and laughed about life's situation. Even David knew that Levy wasn't as nice and perfect as he may seem. David still went along with Levy's fairy tales and how he was this outgoing, intelligent guy. David kept all the bad things that he really wanted to say inside. He even thought about taking Levy's eyes out with the fork he held in his hands. David just couldn't do it. David wanted Levy to die in the worst way possible.

Levy and David took long walks through the park and a canoe ride on the lake. They listened to karaoke at the other end of the Lakeside, underneath a tent full of nice, well-dressed folks.

As they stood around listening to the music Levy, started moving to the rhythm of the music and wrapped his arms around David's neck and said, "I love this song. I like this day and everything about you."

David said, "I do too," and they danced the night away.

David knew that she had to start acting as if she were interested in Levy so that trust would be built between them in order for her to get revenge from her daughter's murder and also the poor people whose lives were taken by this sick, twisted fuck, and she would need to become more manly and show more masculinity.

It was getting late, and they took the canoe back to the other side of the lake.

"How pretty it is out here," Levy said as they paddled down the lake, with trees that lit up like Christmas trees.

"Yes," David said as he laid his head on Levy's shoulder as they canoed the rest of the way.

David and Levy stepped out of the canoe and started gathering their things, and as they were placing the items back into their bag, Levy started trying to make out with David right in the middle of the park.

"I can't," David said as he pulled back. "I can't do this right here, right now, and I don't think it's right timing," David said.

"I understand," Levy replied. "I am sorry. The chemistry is so strong, David. I can't help it. I can't help how bad I want you. I feel like I have known you for a long time to say we just met. I want you, David." He placed his hand on David's face.

David stared at Levy, holding his puke back. "I would rather do this at a more private, romantic place, especially for our first time," David said.

"You're right, babe ," Levy replied. "Do you want to go to your place?"

"No, not tonight," Dave said. "I have to be to a job meeting tomorrow, but we can plan to do something afterward."

"Oh no. Do I have to wait that long, David?"

Eeww, David thought in silence before he said, "I know it's a long wait, but yes, this is a very important meeting."

"I understand," Levy said, "and usually I get very upset when I can't have my wants, but in your case, I would wait for you."

David gave Levy a hug and said that he would call him tomorrow and walked off to his car and drove off.

Before David could make it to his hotel, his phone started ringing. It was Levy; he wanted to know how come David didn't walk him to his car, making sure he got home safe. David said, "I am sorry. I am supertired, just needed to go home and get some rest."

"Oh my god, David. You made me feel as if this was a bad date," Levy said.

"No, I had a great time, and I am sorry, babe . It will not happen again. I will walk you to your vehicle next time," David said.

"Okay, David, I forgive you, now go and get some rest."

When David returned to his room, he became himself, Mrs. Jessie. She looked at herself in the mirror and started crying. "Why, why did it have to be my baby girl?" As she cried, she kept looking at herself in the mirror, rocking back and forth. Mrs. Jessie's mind had gotten so confused she didn't know who she had become. Mrs. Jessie's heart was so heavy right now that she couldn't bear prolonging the situation any longer, but she knew she wanted the job done right. She knew that she wanted Levy to suffer; she wanted Levy to feel the hurt that she felt. She wanted to see Levy's face as he takes his last dying breath as Sasha did.

Mrs. Jessie took a long bath and started making plans for the next day. She even talked out loud to herself, saying, "I can't wait until this sick fuck is dead. I can't wait to see how well he takes pain. I can't wait to see how a bitch cries. I can't wait to see if he can face his own monster that he truly is."

David checked into a nice five-star hotel, and he decorated the room so nice, from the trail of rose petals on the floor that led from the door up to the bed to the champagne that sat chilled in a bucket of ice and the steak dinner that the hotel staff prepared with a side salad and a dinner roll.

How sweet, Levy thought as he turned around and hugged David. "All this for me?" Levy asked.

"Yes," David said, "for all the excitement and fun outings we had."

Levy smiled as he sat down at the dinner table, and his little face had a grin on it from ear to ear.

I want to just cut off his face with that damn steak knife, David said to himself. *All I can do is picture the face of my daughter, Sasha, and how she cried out for help, and I could rescue her. Sometimes I wish it could have been me instead.*

Levy talked and talked, and his words were a big blah, blah, blah, as if his words had no understanding, because David wasn't listening at all.

David noticed Levy getting up from his seat as he made his way to David's end of the table, and he started kissing and feeling on David. David said, "Hold on," as he moved Levy's hand. "What about your wife?" David asked.

Levy moved back. "Wife? How do you know that I have a wife?" Levy asked.

David started looking as if he were lost, with no words to answer Levy's question. "Well," David said, "I noticed the ring the first day I met you."

"Ring?" Levy said.

"Yes, ring, Levy," David said. "I mean, you don't have it on now because you stopped wearing it the minute you met me, but the ring brand is still there."

"Well, David, I see you pay more attention to me than I thought, Mr. Handsome Man."

"Yes, I do," David said. "I paid attention to a lot of things. I paid attention to you the first day I met you. I mean, your attractiveness caught my attention. That nice tight ass of yours and those cut-up muscular arms of yours. I mean, I was hoping you were single."

"Look, David," Levy said. "I am married, but there's something about you that's different. No one ever caught my attention like you did. My dick is aroused every time I get around you, and when I talk to you on the phone, this ball of happiness runs through me. I feel so loved, and it's a type of feeling that I cannot explain. David, telling you I was married would have just ran you off, but I had to see what was so different about you, what was the spark that started my flames and led them to be so high and hot for you, because I never knew anyone that made me feel that way."

David smiled at Levy, and in David's mind, he thought, *Maybe because I am a woman. Women spark men's flames. I'm not sure how that man-to-man stuff works, but I do know that I will have his cold, cruel, and desperate heart in my hands.* David started rubbing Levy's chest and kissing him, telling Levy that he knew that exact same feeling. David put his hands down his pants and started jacking off his dick.

Levy was enjoying it, as David can tell by the face expressions and the clinching of his thighs. "Suck it, baby," Levy said to David. "Suck it. It needs your lips on the tip of it."

David got on his knees and started sucking his dick. Levy started moaning louder and louder, saying, "Yes, baby. I like it just like that."

For a minute, I could bear having his pink dick in my mouth, but I have to get him to trust me enough, and I need to get his mind to be focused right on me. By the way, I am a woman. I know my shit. No man can do a better job than a real woman, and his dumb ass wonders why he can't explain that feeling that he has, that spark that lit up.

Levy started saying that he didn't feel so good and that he felt dizzy. David told him to lie down on the bed and close his eyes and try to relax. Before Levy could figure out what was wrong with him, he passed out.

Everything that David had planned came into play. David took all of Levy's clothes off and handcuffed him to the bed. David then sat along the bedside until Levy awake. When Levy's eyes was open, he looked around the room and asked why everything looked so blurred, and David said in a woman's voice, "The drugs will wear off in thirty minutes."

"Who the fuck are you?" Levy asked. "And where the fuck is David."

"David? Don't worry. David is okay," Mrs. Jessie said as she started laughing out loud.

"You don't know me. You're making a big mistake, bitch," Levy yelled.

"Oh, I know you very well mister," Mrs. Jessie said. "I know you well enough to know that you are a married man and you like to lie. You want things your way. You're controlling, you murdered your ex-husband and the staff at the hospital, and you murdered the wrong daughter."

Levy got quiet as he lift his head up and said, "That whore daughter of yours slept with my husband. She walked around as if she didn't have a fucking care in the world that he was married. She walked around as if fucking people's men was okay to do. No, no, no, it was not okay to do!" Levy yelled as he cried out. "I loved my husband, and I said nobody was going to ever, ever take him from me. I told Jared when we got married we will be together until death do us part, and I meant that, and death do us part."

"Yeah, Levy, is that so, but there is only one problem." She kneeled over him. "My daughter wasn't in that vow, you sick fuck," Mrs. Jessie said as she pierced his nipples with a hole puncher.

Levy screamed loudly because of the pain caused by the dullness of the metal. Levy's vision became clearer, and he noticed David laughing, pacing up and down the room, as he lay down listening to the sound of a woman coming out of David's mouth. Levy looked so confused as he yelled to David, "Who the fuck are you, and what the fuck do you want? Dude, you should know how it feels. Come on, man, you felt our love connection. You saw the type of person that I am. All I wanted was a happy life. I got my first love taken from me by the hands of my mother. I wasn't gonna let the second one taken. I just couldn't, David." Levy cried out.

Mrs. Jessie said, "I am your worst fucking nightmare." She duct-taped Levy's mouth to keep him quiet. "I am the mother who will know that her daughter's killer gets what he deserves. I am a mother who had someone taken away from her by the hand of a twisted-ass killer. Revenge is what I want." Mrs. Jessie took a knife and started carving words in Levy's skin. One word said *devil,* and another one said *sick.* The other words said *lies, murderer,* and *twisted fuck.* You could see the veins popping out Levy's neck as his pained red face drained with heavy tears.

"You know, Levy, some people become someone that they never plan to become. People's minds become twisted all the time, and the crazy part about it, people seek other people to help find the solution to their problem, but the problem starts at home. The sickness starts at home, and instead of seeking professional help, like you, instead of getting help, you just feed off the sickness, and you became sicker," Mrs. Jessie said. "You know, I remember Sasha when she was just a little baby. Her little hand that gripped around my index finger, the smell of her infant milk on her blankets when I washed. I remember her smile, her laughter, and her voice calling *mom* late at night when she was having nightmares. I remember helping her ride her first bike, and I had to chase behind her because she didn't know how to stop." Mrs. Jessie's eyes poured tears while she talked about Sasha.

"Seeing someone grow from this precious little baby girl who is up doing the night and sleep the day away, from a baby to a talking toddler, who had colors and markers all over my walls, to a teenager who did what most typical teenager did, the senior prom where I dressed her so nicely in this elegant mermaid gown. Oh, how she looked so beautiful." Mrs. Jessie couldn't stop crying as she talked about the raising of Sasha up until her death.

"Tell me, Levy, why couldn't you just move on? Why couldn't you just sit, talk it out with your husband? How come you had to take her life? She was a human being. You know we as people make mistakes. I doubt if she even knew he was married. I doubt if she even knew any of your situation, Levy."

Mrs. Jessie ripped the tape off Levy's mouth and said, "I want to know, did you make her suffer?"

Levy just stared at Mrs. Jessie with his red, watery eyes, as he turned his head, looking in the other direction away from Jessie. Levy then said as he started crying, "I tied her down to a bed post. I torched her, slapped her, pissed on her. Sasha cried out for help, asking who I was, why I was doing that to her. She was so beautiful." Levy cried. "And then I raped her, put a knife into her numerous times as her blood exited her body like a thick, heavy, and fast waterfall," Levy said as he cried, giving up on himself, knowing he was going to die.

Mrs. Jessie cried even more, until she could cry anymore. "Levy, you walk around as if you didn't have a care in this world. Hell, you even created yourself a whole new family, kids and a husband, but you know the fuck-up thing about this whole situation, Levy? What makes you better than Sasha? What makes you different? You're married now, Levy, and here you are, falling in love, creeping around, trying to get some dick, when you got dick at home. You are a married man that said until death do you part again, and this time it's you. How do you think your husband would feel if he found out, Levy?" Mrs. Jessie asked. Then she said, "You're doing what Sasha did, so should your husband feel like you did when you found out Jared cheated on you. I mean, you're in the same boat. All those horrible things you did to her," Mrs. Jessie said, and then she said it again as she was crying, "All those horrible things that you did to her." Mrs. Jessie then asked Levy, "How did she take her last dying breath?"

He cried out, "While looking in the mirror."

Mrs. Jessie took the mirror off the room wall and placed it in front of Levy. Mrs. Jessie said, "Nothing you did is different from Sasha, when you're doing the exact same thing, but only you're the married man that's cheating on your husband, and you had no care in the world while doing it." Mrs. Jessie laughed as if she had done lost it, and then she looked at Levy and said, "Now the shoe is on the other foot. I am going to take five things from you, Levy. One, your dick that you used to rape my daughter; two, your eyes that you saw through when you watched my daughter die; three, your ears that heard my daughter's cry out for help; four, your heart that you didn't use to even care or feel sorry for her. You can be heartless, along with the devil." She carved his heart out his chest as he took his last breath while looking in the mirror.

Mrs. Jessie packed up all her things and cleaned up the room real neat, leaving no marks, no fingerprints, or nothing behind that would tie her to a murder.

She returned back home, and she became herself again. She read in the newspaper that a body was found inside a hotel room and that they did not have a suspect. She also read that the clerk gave the police a description of a man that he was last seen with by the name David. The hotel cameras were not working at the time, so that left the police with no evidence, only the body that was torn apart. The missing pieces were not discovered at the scene but were later discovered by the mother of the corps in their mail box with a letter that read, "He should have paid attention to him better." Mrs. Jessie heard a few months later the mother hung herself. Luckily, the children that they adopted were placed with new parents, two sick fucks off the streets.

Mrs. Jessie was back to normal. She still held speeches and talks to people about life and tried her best to lead them to better themselves. Mrs. Jessie still worked in the investigation department and was stress-free, knowing that her daughter was at rest.

Sasha can now be at peace, and so can I. By the way, number five, I got revenge.

Printed in the United States
by Baker & Taylor Publisher Services